Beckett

ROBINSON DESTRUCTION BOOK 4

KATHI S. BARTON

This is a work of fiction. Names, characters, places, and incidents are products of the author's imagination or are used fictitiously and are not to be construed as real. Any resemblance to actual events, locations, organizations, or persons, living or dead, is entirely coincidental.

World Castle Publishing, LLC
Pensacola, Florida
Copyright © Kathi S. Barton 2020
Paperback ISBN: 9781953271501
eBook ISBN: 9781953271518
First Edition World Castle Publishing, LLC, December 21, 2021
http://www.worldcastlepublishing.com

Licensing Notes

Cover: Karen Fuller
Editor: Maxine Bringenberg

Chapter 1

Houston finished up the paperwork that had been piling up on his desk while they'd been gone. Three of the most fabulous weeks skipping around the world, and he'd not wanted to come home. He didn't think he could have stayed forever, but a few more weeks wouldn't have been too bad.

Looking up when he heard a noise, he smiled at Sam when he came into his office and flopped down on the chair. Looking up at him again, he nearly had a massive heart attack when he saw his face. Taking a deep breath before speaking, he asked him what had happened.

"The school nurse said it was my fault. It wasn't. I have to have a meeting with her and my grandpa tomorrow." Houston asked him why he was stitched up. "This kid, he's in a higher grade than I am. He said I was stupid. I'm not. But when I tried to prove to him that I was smart, that ticked him off something terrible, and he used his notebook to beat me up. Why? Why does everyone have to think that beating someone up is a good way to solve something?"

"I don't know. But I'd say you're going to have to talk to your aunt about those bruises too. Did you know she's here today?" He looked around like his aunt was going to jump out of the woodwork at any second. "Who did the work, Sam? Was it the school nurse?"

"Yes. She said it was too distracting for her to fill out paperwork on me while I had this gaping hole in my face. I wanted her to call Uncle Thatcher or Uncle Dawson, but she told me they more than likely had better things to do than to come down there and mess with me." Sam looked upset. "They'd not think that, would they, Uncle Houston?"

"Never. I'm going to contact them now and tell them they need to have a look at you. Are you hurt anywhere else?" When Sam stood up, Houston had a very difficult time holding onto his tiger. The kid looked like he'd been run over a couple of times, then once more just for the fun of it. "Did the school nurse see these as well, son?"

"She didn't let me show her. I told her I was hurting, but she said that since I'd started the fight, I'd have to deal with a little pain. Nurse Calendar sent me back to class after she fixed my face. Uncle Houston, do you think the aunts will have a hissy fit and kill her?" It was tempting for Houston to run out and do just that himself. "They sure do get powerful mad when they figure someone is getting the shaft, don't they?"

"They do at that. I'm assuming they didn't notify your grandparents either, did they?" Sam started to shake his head and put his hands to his temples. "Right. All right, we're going to the hospital. And I'm calling the police as well as the family. There are some important laws being broken right now, and I want someone's ass to be roasted for it."

Sam started to laugh but stopped. Houston was so pissed off right now he had to take in and let out several long breaths before he could speak. Yelling for Tru because it gave him a way to let off a little of the steam, he was glad to see her almost as soon as he finished saying her name. While she fussed over Sam with him telling her what he'd told Houston, he reached out to his family.

I'm going to take Sam to the hospital. Would someone please take his grandparents? I don't want them thinking the worst. It is bad but not life threatening. At least not his life. He told them what he'd heard from Sam. *She didn't notify anyone and put the worst looking stitches in his cheek and forehead that I've —*

She didn't have permission to do that, did she? Houston told Thatcher that, as he was saying, he didn't believe she'd even called anyone. *I'll meet you at the emergency room. I'd say bring him here to the clinic, but I think this needs to be done with the police involved. The police are going to have to question Sam. Is he going to be all right with that?*

I would think so. He didn't have any trouble telling me. I think that with him having Tru there, he's going to be a little better. She will also be able to make sure he's not bullied.

Thatch thought that was a great idea. *He's pretty beat up, guys. And the longer he sits here, the more the bruises are showing up. And his back. Christ, it looks to me like he was dragged through gravel. Or was beaten with a whip. I've not asked him which. I'm barely holding on here as it is.*

Tru sat in the back seat with Sam and Jacob. He could tell that Jacob was upset, but he was trying very hard to be brave for his brother and aunt. Every time Houston got a spare second, he would turn and speak to the younger one. Jacob was the most tender little guy he knew. Something occurred to him while he was sitting at a light, and he turned to ask him about it.

"You've not had any trouble with the school, have you, buddy?" When he didn't answer right away, Houston glanced at Tru. "Jacob, is there trouble with your teachers as well? We don't want to have you suffering if you don't have to."

"Tell them, Jake. You have to tell them too." So, his brother knew as well. This was beginning to be serious now. Pulling over into the grocery store lot, he waited on Jacob to see what he had to say. "I told them. Now you have to do it. It's not right like he said."

"Some of the other kids knock me around when I'm going to my lunchroom or class." Houston knew it was more than that, so he waited for him to get things in his head organized so he could tell him. "I don't tell the teachers anymore. They said I'm lucky anyone wants to have me around them. That my dad is a womanizer and that my mom didn't even want us. They were going to sell us off, so we're nothing to anyone. I don't know what that is, but I think it's a bad word."

"It is the way they're using it. Houston, please take us to the hospital. Please." Tru touched his mind, and he could almost feel her anger. *I'm not going to go to the school. I'm not going to go to the school and kill every last one of those fucking bitches.*

I know just what you mean. He pulled out into traffic again and told her what he'd done. *I didn't want your parents to freak out, so Beckett is going to pick them up so they don't drive. It's bad enough that they've hurt Sam, but Jacob is about the sweetest kid in the world. Why would anyone want to hurt him too?*

I'm so pissed right now. I don't know how you're driving so calmly. I'd be driving too fast and running every red light. He told her he was having a hard time of it as well, but he was concentrating hard on driving safely. *Not me. Those fuckers are going to pay for this. You wait and see.*

Both his brothers were at the hospital when they arrived. Thatcher took one look at Sam and ordered an entire set of X-rays, as well as a CAT scan. Dawson had to keep breathing deeply in and out to keep his cat under control. The Justices showed up just as his parents did. Hell was going to be paid if the looks on their faces were any indication. Then Andrew, chief of police, showed up with two deputies.

"Don't say a word." He smiled at Tru when she got up in his face. "I want to do this by the books, and if I have to arrest you to keep you from telling my men what to do, you know I'll do it. You have to lay low because everyone is going to say you've forced my hand in this. All right?"

"Yes. I understand. I don't have to like it, but I do understand. Wait until you see them, Andrew. They're a fucking mess." He said he'd sent two of his men to pick up not only the nurse at the grade school but also the principal and the lady that ran the desk in the office. "Thank you. I do appreciate you doing this."

When the other two women showed up, Andrew told them the same thing. Houston thought he was lucky to have been the one to tell them. He'd have not wanted to be anywhere near any of them right now. They were as pissed off as he'd ever seen them.

A message came from Jacob to have him come and see him.

"Hey, buddy. What's wrong?" He'd been crying, and it hurt Houston in ways he couldn't explain to anyone if asked. "Your grandparents are out there. Do you want them to come and see you too?"

"I'm not going to prison, am I? I don't want to be there where the other parents are that gave birth to us." They'd decided that even though Trudy and Blake had adopted their grandsons, they'd continue to call them their grandparents. "That kid that hits me all the time, he told me that if I told on him, I'd go to prison just like the other parents did. And the nurse, she told me I'd better be keeping my mouth zipped, or I'd be just another name in a book. I don't know what that means, but I don't think she meant it in a good way, do you? Don't tell my grandparents. I don't want them to have a stroke or something and leave us behind. We do worry about them all the time, Sam and me."

"That's very good of you, but I think you need to keep them in the loop from now on. But no, I don't think she meant that as anything but a bad word. But you're not going anywhere except home when they release you. The police are here too. They're going to ask you some questions about what happened. Jacob, you tell them the truth about all this, even if it embarrasses you or makes you feel bad. I swear to you, nothing is going to happen to you or Sam." He asked if his aunt could be there with him. "Yes. She'll like that. But don't let her yell at the police too much. You and I both know she's a little protective of the two of you."

"She sure is." They both smiled. While he was telling him about the work he was doing at home, Tru and Andrew showed up. Houston stood up to leave. "Uncle Houston, can you make sure that my brother is all right? And tell Grandma and Grandpa that I'm all right? I don't want them to worry too much. They've been really good to me and Sam."

Houston said he would and had to leave the little area quickly. He was so close to sobbing about how much he loved these kids that he was sure he'd be a soggy mess before talking to the Justices. Finding them in one of the private rooms in the emergency room, Houston told them what he knew and what had been done about it.

"Thatch was in here a few seconds ago. He's going to find out what he can about Sam. I didn't know any of this was going on." Houston assured Blake that he'd not known either. "It does explain a lot, though. The last week or so, the two of them have been spending a lot of time in their rooms. I was thinking they were regretting that we took them. But now, I think they were nursing their wounds. Don't you?"

"Someone told Jacob that he'd end up in the same prison as his parents if he were to tell anyone." Trudy started crying softly when he told them that. "Did Sam come and ask you if he could come to our house?"

"We weren't home when he got there. We told him so long as he gets his homework finished up, he could always go to one of your homes. I found his bookbag outside of the house like he'd never even gone in when your brother showed up to bring us here. I think he'd had enough and decided to get you and Tru involved. I hate to ask you this, but why didn't the two of them come to us?" Houston told him what the boys, both of them, had said to them. "They think that we'll have a heart attack and leave them? I guess I can understand that. I went to the doctor the other day, and neither of them believes I got a clean bill of health. I've been sort of acting my age lately. You know, moaning and groaning about every little thing. I was doing it just to be funny. I won't do that anymore."

"No, I don't think you should. Not until the two of them are a little more secure with you and themselves."

Houston looked up when the elevator dinged for this floor. "When you see Sam, just know that he's getting the best of care. Thatcher and Dawson are working together to make sure of that."

Sam was laying back on the gurney when he was brought out of the elevator. He thought that every time he saw him, he looked a little worse for wear. Neither Blake nor Trudy moved to follow him back to a room. He thought they were just as upset as Sam was right now. In pain too—a different sort of pain, but still hurting.

Houston followed Dawson when he went by him. He didn't pepper him with questions like he wanted to but just stayed with him. As soon as he entered the little room with Sam, he got word that Jacob was going up for X-rays as well. Dawson sat down on one of the little stools that he moved closer to Sam's bed when he was ready to speak.

"Do you want this like a man, or do you want me to sugar coat it a little for you?" Sam looked at Houston, and he told him that Dawson was good at both ways. "I'm a sight better than your aunts would have been. You tell me, and I'll tell you what I've found out. Thatcher is working with your brother if you're going to ask me."

"I was. He's hurt too." Dawson said he'd found that out. "I want to be a man about it, but I'm still afraid. I didn't start this fight, Uncle Dawson. I swear I didn't."

"I know that, son. We all know that. All right?" Sam nodded. "You have a fractured wrist and a couple of cracked ribs." Houston had to sit or lean onto something, or he might well have fallen over. "Also, this is going to suck, but I'm going to have to redo the stitches that were put in. Do you know if she washed them out before she did it, Sam?"

"No. She told me I was making a mess and distracting her, so she laid me down on the bed and put them in. It hurt too." Dawson looked at him before Sam spoke again. "I don't want to have to go back to that school. I don't care if I have to be a deadbeat. I just don't want to hurt anymore."

A nurse came in and gave Sam something to relax him. It was enough that it also knocked him out. Dawson had to leave the little room before he could work on Sam—he was that angry. Houston was close to hunting down the woman who had done this and tearing her apart. That wouldn't be a figure of speech either.

~*~

Tru sat with the boys after they'd been admitted. They were both in the same bed in Sam's room. She was glad for it. The two of them needed each other now more than ever. Sam was still out from earlier, and Jacob had been given something as well. The two of them were so stressed out having to deal with this on their own, Dawson said he didn't think that either of them had gotten a good night's sleep lately.

She was still sitting there with the boys when her mom came into the room.

"I feel like the worst kind of parent to these two." Tru told her it had nothing at all to do with her and Dad. "I know that in my head, but my heart isn't having any of it. Do you suppose this has been going on from the very beginning? Them being bullied, I mean?"

"I don't think so. They've been going there for a month and a half. What I think happened is that the kids were having their fun with them, and when the teachers didn't say anything, they went for the big time. The kid that hurt Sam is going to be put in jail. I don't know for how long, but long enough that he sees the error of his ways. Five boys had been hurting them, with the encouragement of their parents. I'm taking care of them." She expected her mom to tell her not to kill them, but all she said was good. "Mom, they didn't want you and Dad to worry. They have it in their head that if anything happens to the two of you, they're going to be taken to prison to live with their parents. I don't know who told them that bunch of bullshit, but you can bet that I'm going to find out."

"I hope you make them see the error of their ways as well." She put her hand on Jacob's head as it rested on his brother's pillow. "They look so tiny right now. I thought they were beginning to come out of their shells around us. Not that they've been terrible to us. In fact, they've been as good as gold. We couldn't have asked for better children. But I always felt that they were holding back some part of themselves. I wish it had only been that they were not trusting us in some way. Holding back on being hurt like they have been makes me feel like I failed them."

"There is no telling what Shasta told them about the

two of you. Or me, for that matter. She wouldn't have been happy with anything that we supposedly did to her by not giving her money or anything else." Mom said she'd not thought of that. "Also, they would have heard her bitching with Mike about all of us, and you know as well as I do that kids hear more than anyone thinks they do. I can't imagine how much shit we're going to have to fix because of them."

"I should have thought of that myself. I used to tell Shasta that she shouldn't say things like she did in front of them. That they'd hear her and take it to heart. When I think of all the things they heard about you when you were away, I could just scream. I'm so sorry, honey." Tru told her she didn't care that she had made her peace with Shasta hating her. "When you told me she said that she hated you, I could have just sobbed. My goodness, when I think of all the things I'm finding out now about her and Mike and what they did, I want to bury my head in the sand. You were right about telling us to never lie to the boys about anything that we find out. It's difficult at times, but we do it. Simply because we want them to be able to handle anything that comes along."

There was a very timid knock at the door, and a little boy came into the room. He looked lost for a second, then saw the boys. Clark, she thought his name was, and she asked him if he was there to see the boys.

"Yes, ma'am. I am. I didn't know they was having trouble. I'm going to a different school now, and we don't see each other as much. I'm doing my homework."

Tru told him that was wonderful and moved so he could sit next to the bed to see them. "I surely wish I'd known what was going on. I would have been in trouble for them. They're my best friends, you know."

Overnight, after one night of staying with the boys, Clark really had become a different child. He started studying his homework, paying attention in class, and was no longer a bully. In fact, Tru had heard that he was making a name for himself, telling others to straighten up their act. Tru stepped into the hallway while Clark talked quietly to her mom. She'd been missing the little boy too.

Rogen was coming down the hallway, almost as if she knew she'd be standing there. "I have some news. Want to go and get something to drink with me so I can talk to you?" Tru asked her if she could tell her mom. "Yes. If she wants to come too, that's fine with me."

Mom didn't want to leave the boys. Plus, she and Clark were talking about his new school. Tru would bet anything that by the end of the day, not only would Sam and Jacob be pulled from the other school, but they'd be joining their best friend at his.

"I've found the video of the nurse putting the stitches in his head. Christ, she didn't even give him anything for the fucking pain. You can see him gripping the side of the bed hard enough to leave an impression on it. Fucker is going to pay." She asked her if she'd been picked up yet. "Yes. Thankfully, or not so much, without any incident. The principal was telling the officers that picked her up that she had nothing to do with the failure to report. I didn't know that was a state rule until then. Did you?"

"Yes. I did a stint as a teacher once. They have all kinds of rules like that. Also, that a nurse cannot administer pain medications to any child unless an adult that is related to them is there. She gave Jacob an aspirin yesterday when he was in the office for his injuries." Rogen asked her if she'd heard about what had happened to Jacob. "Houston told me that he has a sprained wrist as well as some deep bruises. His back is torn up like his brother's as well. Apparently, the teachers are using flyswatters and a smallish whip on them when they're called upon in class. Not to answer questions, but to have them stand up and tell them about their parents. The boys wouldn't do that, and it would make the teacher pissy enough that she took her frustrations out on them."

"I have had them arrested too. The entire school is closed down for a few weeks. Long enough for me to get the lowdown on all of them. I did hear from one of the kids that the custodian would hide the boys in his closet so they'd not have to go out on the playground. That is where most of this shit happened. I'm so sorry, Tru. I know you well enough by now to know that this is killing you inside."

"It is. But more than that, I want to hunt them down and take them out. Not even say a word to them, just kill and move on." She looked around when she realized they weren't alone in the cafeteria. "What have you figured out so far? I'm sure you didn't bring me down here for a glass of the nastiest tea I've ever drank."

"No—not only that, anyway. And I'm sort of glad your mom decided not to come. I have two things to tell you that are going to make you madder than you already are. Jacob's teacher is an ex-con—for child abuse. How she got by the background test is something else that I'm looking into. You can bet that heads are going to roll with that one." Tru asked if she could take care of her. "Seriously, it might well come to that. I'm looking into things. The second thing I have to tell you is that your nephews aren't the first to get treated this way. Not nearly as bad, but almost so. I have six grown men coming to me about the treatment they got while in school there. It's going to close this school up faster than anything when it gets out that they covered things up. Same principal, same nurse."

"What else?" Rogen told her she was working up to it. When Anna joined them, she turned a file that she had in her hand over to Tru. Tru opened the file and stared at the pictures she saw there before looking up at her friend. "Is this who I think it is?"

"It is if you think that's the president of these here United States. He was a child in one of the earlier schools that these two worked at early in their career of harming children. I put in a call to him about it, and I'm waiting for a callback. He's running the country, I was told, and couldn't be bothered. I'd like to hear what he has to say about that when he finds out what has happened here." They both laughed, and Anna came back from getting a bag of chips and some juice. "I was bringing her up to date on the names of some of their victims. Especially our president. He still has a hard on about having us work personally with him. I believe that's just too much power to give to one person. If he keeps hounding me about it, I'm going to up and quit. See how he likes that. The fucking bastard isn't taking no for an answer."

"Word has it that these two change their name and move on when things start to get hot. Someone warns them that there is going to be a police call, and they both skip town. They're roomies, not lovers that I can find, but they do live in the same household most of the time. Not this time, for some reason that I'm looking into, but they do spend a great deal of time together. Anyway, have you tried this new brand of chips? They taste like horse hay." Tru was getting used to Anna's way of drifting in a conversation if she had things that she didn't think you'd be happy with. "I have seventeen people that are going to be given their summons to appear in the morning. Everyone at the school, including the cooks, is going to have to appear at some point when this hits the court system."

"Do you think they were all involved?" Anna told her they were and why. "So just knowing about the abuse is going to get them shit canned. Good. I'm betting that in a few weeks, there are going to be a lot of people demanding their money back. I think my parents are wishing they'd not put them in this private school now. I know I didn't even look at anything about it when I should have. I take some of the blame for that."

"As I said, the school will close down, and then maybe—and that's a big maybe—it will reopen when they have a new set of teachers. I was going to ask Morgan if he'd mind helping us with that for a few months. Not teaching, but just interviews." Tru asked if she thought he'd do it. "I do now. Perhaps not before this happened, but he will now."

Nodding, the three of them were still talking when Houston joined them. Her dad was with him, and they seemed to be having a very serious conversation. However, when they sat down, they talked about how the boys were holding up well and would more than likely be going home in the morning.

"My parents are going to help with some of the care they're both going to need. Not a great deal, but Thatcher wants them to have a good bit of fun for the next couple of weeks. After they heal up a little. Then they're going to go to the pack school with their buddy Clark." Tru had forgotten about that and was glad that Houston mentioned it. She knew that Clark was going to a different school and that his mom worked for the packhouse. Tru had simply forgotten. "There will be a lot of arrests over the next few days. Even some parents are going to be taken in concerning this. The two main people are in jail now. I've never been so glad of someone being arrested as I am the two of them." Everyone agreed.

When Tru made her way back to the room, she thought about what other things had been in the file.

There were pictures of other abused children, each picture accompanied by all the information of the now adults. The one that bothered her the most was the one of the young boy that looked to be about seven. His death certificate said he'd committed suicide when he couldn't handle what they were doing to him anymore.

Tru was going to make sure that no matter what happened, the boys were going to be all right mentally. She might talk to her parents about having them see someone now before they got in any deeper. Making herself a note on it, she was happy to find the boys both awake and talking to Clark. Kids could bounce back from just about anything, she thought.

Chapter 2

Allen watched his sister. He knew she was pissed off, but talking to her about it would only put him in her sites to take it out on. So he sat at the table and read the newspaper in bits and pieces. When she finally turned around and looked at him, it broke his heart to see that she'd been crying. Getting up, he pulled her into his arms and held her.

"They had to go and hurt those little boys, didn't they?" He didn't bother asking her to give him more details. They'd been living together for the last four years, and he knew her well enough to know she'd get to it. "I lost my job today. Not lost it, but I've been put on leave pending an investigation. What the hell do they hope to find? That I helped them abuse the students? I didn't even know anything was going on—they've got me chasing my tail all the time. I'm supposed to be a teacher. I went to school for a long time to be one. And what do they have me doing? Slinging hash."

"Hash?" She glared at him. "Sorry. I'm supposed to be supportive. But you have to admit, there have been some strange things going on there. Even you noticed it."

"I'm not blind, you idiot. I was trying to keep out of shit until I was a teacher." Allen wanted to tease her into a better mood by pointing out that teachers didn't say shit, but he was much too close to her. "I wish I could have been able to see what was going on with them. It's bad enough that the cooks are fucking with the deliveries of food."

"What? The newspaper doesn't mention anything about the cafeteria. They only mention some children that have been hurt by the staff." Allie pulled the newspaper to her and started reading the article. Allen started pulling things out of the fridge for their dinner. "I've been to the police department twice now. I can't get in to see anyone about my supposed interview. When you were working, I had a little time. Now that neither of us are, we're going to be hurting before long. There have been days lately that I wished we'd not moved out here. They're a very close-knit town here, aren't they?"

"Yes. I went to the clinic to see if I could get in for us to have our allergy shots set up, and they said I'd have to have a full background check. For a clinic? I've had one as a teacher—wait, a hash slinger—but you'll need one, I guess." He'd had one when he was in the service. Allen didn't mention it, however. She was still pissy. "What I wouldn't do right now for a good paying full-time job. Or a nice wealthy husband. I don't care if he's an old man. I'd like to have security in my life. Wouldn't you?"

"I don't think I'd enjoy being married to an old man. I don't care how wealthy or old he was. Not going to happen for me. As for getting a full-time job? I've been looking, sweetie." She told him she knew he had. "But I do understand what you're saying. It would be nice to have a secure place to live, work, and be able to retire when we're old enough."

After having their dinner, they planned what their next move would be. In the morning, he was going to go to the new hospital and see what they were hiring for. Allen had been a medic in the service, but those kinds of jobs, he was finding out, didn't switch out as well as he had hoped when he'd been discharged. Allen looked down at his leg and wondered daily what would have happened had he just laid there in the field and not called out for anyone to come and get him. Allie would certainly be better off.

At six, they did their nightly ritual. First, the local news, then the world news. After that, they'd watch Jeopardy, then another game show until eight. Allie would turn off the television, he'd pick up the paper where he'd left off, and she'd go and do some online classwork in her *pretend* classroom. He was sure that if she was ever to get herself a teaching job, she'd have all her yearly schedules filled out until the end of time. Allen's heart broke for the two of them.

They'd been orphans, the two of them. They weren't related by blood but did have the same adoptive parents.

Bill and Sherri Langley had taken them both when they'd only gone to the place for a little boy. Allie, they told them, was an added bonus. He thought they had been right about that.

Their parents hadn't had a great deal of material things nor money. However, they had loved them. Neither of them cared what they didn't have as much as other children did because they'd been chosen, not born to their family. That hadn't worked as well as they'd hoped it would when they'd been in school that year. But once he started to tower over most of the kids in the school, the kids left the two of them alone.

Allen was six years older than Allie. He'd been ten when they'd been adopted, and her only four. Even to this day, he could never find out why she'd not been adopted from the very first day she'd been at the home. The rumors he'd heard about little Jane Doe number fifty-three were that no one wanted a redhead as a child. She also had the most beautiful green eyes he'd ever seen. Something about them having the power to look into your soul. Bullshit.

"I'm going to head to bed. I've been getting up so early to go to work that I'd very much like to sleep in until I just can't sleep anymore." Allen knew she'd be up at five in the morning, as she had been since she was a child. "What time are you going to the hospital tomorrow to apply? Maybe I can find something to do. I do know how to sling hash better than anyone I know."

"I was going to be there at nine. They start interviews

at ten. I want to look the place over. It's supposed to be this state-of-the-art hospital. The emergency room, which is already up and running, has been featured in all kinds of articles about its lifesaving equipment. It's also the only privately owned hospital in the state, I guess."

Allie told him she'd go too, and he told her goodnight. After she went to her room, he pulled out the help wanted section of the paper. There were a pitiful number of ads for the area. He supposed the hospital being in the area would bring in more businesses, and after that, more people. Allen thought it would ruin the small-town atmosphere around here. It was one of the reasons that they'd picked this area for its small population.

Marking the three that were in the paper, he pulled out his laptop, which he was sure every time he turned it on would die on him. Allen filled out the applications and hoped for the best. For the time being, he could only work jobs that had him off his feet. He was still healing from the raid he'd been in on that took the lives of so many other officers that day.

Putting the paper down, he thought about what he could have done differently that day. Nothing came to mind. He'd been over and over the situation ten times a day since he'd woken up in the field hospital. They'd been able to save his life and his leg, but he'd not been able to stay a serviceman—too much muscle damage, he'd been told. Not only that, but he still had terrible nightmares about it. Debilitating dreams that would make him scream loud enough for Allie to hear from her room down the hall from his.

The knock at the door startled him. Getting up, he glanced at the clock on the wall as he walked by it. It was well after one in the morning. Allen hadn't realized he'd been sitting there for that long. He looked out the upper window to see a man standing there. Instead of opening the door, he asked him what he wanted. The man turned to him with a huge smile.

"I'm broken down. Not only that, but I also seem to have left my cell phone at work. I know you don't know me, but I'm hoping you've heard of my family. I'm Beckett Robinson." Allen told him he had, but he still wasn't going to open the door. "I don't blame you one bit for that. If you could just sort of slip me a phone out that I can use, I'll put it back on the stoop after I call for help. I don't want to disturb my family this late at night."

Allie stumbled out of her room just as he was going back to the table for his phone. Before he could tell her who was at the door, she pulled it open and asked the man standing there what the ever-loving fuck he wanted.

"I'm broken down." Allie, forever taking things the literal way, told him he looked like he was in one piece to her. "My car. My car is broken down, and I don't want to have to disturb my family."

"But it's all right for you to disturb strangers." He just grinned, and she told him to either come in or stay out. She was going back to bed. "My brother will take care of you. But if you hurt him, I'm going to hunt you down and murder you. I've had a shitty day, and I'm not in a great fucking mood."

The door to her room slammed shut. Allen, embarrassed at his sister's rudeness, told Beckett he was sorry. The man turned his gaze from where Allie had gone with what looked to him like a great effort. Beckett only smiled at him and told him it was fine now. Everything was just as fine as rain.

"Yes, well, you might not think so if you plan on harming either of us. She might be tiny, but she's meaner than a rattlesnake when she thinks someone is taking advantage of either of us."

Beckett took the phone from him and opened it up. Allen went into the kitchen area to put his computer away. His gun was now safely in the side cushion of the couch.

That would be written on his headstone. "Here lies Allen Langley. He died young because he was too stupid to know that in order to save himself, he needed to keep his gun on his person." It was too long, but he could see his sister making the stone cutter put every last word on it. He realized then that Beckett was staring at him.

"I'm sorry. I zoned out there for a second. What is it you said?" He repeated his question. "Shifters? I guess we are aware of them. I don't know if I actually know any. I mean, it's not something I've done before. Asking a person what they are. Are you one?"

"Yes. I'm a tiger. My family is." He'd heard that at some point, that the Robinsons were tigers. Telling him he could have a seat, Beckett sat down and laughed. "I'm sort of giddy right now. I know that sounds like a stupid statement, a grown man being giddy, but that's what I am. I've found my mate."

"No. I don't think so. I mean, I have nothing against a man preferring a man in a relationship. However, I don't swing that way. Thanks, but no thanks." Beckett laughed again and said it was his sister. "Allie? Well, I'm sure I can tell you right now that you're not her type. She was just telling me tonight that she wants to marry a very old man that has money to leave her. Allie isn't a gold digger or anything like that. We've been struggling since I was discharged from the service, and you just don't fit her bill right now. But you're welcome to try. Be warned, however, that she's a mean as a snake in the grass when cornered."

"My brothers' mates are like that. But loving as well. I'm very sorry that you're struggling. I can help you with that. Not struggling, but to not struggle." Beckett laughed. "I'm sort of out of my element here. I expected to find my mate, but later down the line, I guess. What can you tell me about her?"

"Nothing. I mean, I could. I know her better than she knows herself. But that's not something I'd feel comfortable doing without her permission." Beckett said that was a good thing. He'd not thought of that. "She's only just lost her job today. I'd like to tell you that's what put her out of sorts tonight, but that's not all of it. Allie has wanted to be a teacher for a long time—since we were adopted. But the school that she was trying to get a teaching position in closed up today. She wasn't a teacher there. They took her on as a cook. She can't. Cook, I mean. So she slings hash there. That's what she calls— Now I'm babbling. I'm sorry."

"Don't be." Beckett leaned back in the seat he was in. "As I said, my family is the Robinsons. And we're tigers. I also want you to know that I'd never harm her or hurt her. Not on purpose. I have a feeling, however, that she is going to fit right in with my family. You as well."

Allen didn't know about that, but the man was looney if he thought that he or Allie would just say, "Okay, you're related to us now, we'll follow along like sheep." Neither he nor Allie had ever been the norm when they could branch out on their own if they thought their way was better. Usually, with Allie in charge, it was. Allie was not only smart but street smart.

"I woke my brother Houston. He's the only one I know that goes to bed late most of the time. Of course, this time, he didn't. But he's in a good mood too. I told him about Allie." Allen asked him if that was a good idea since she didn't know yet. "Probably not. But I wanted someone in the family to know. He was mad that I woke him. That smoothed things over a bit for me."

When someone knocked at the door, Beckett asked if he could get it. Allen's leg was bothering him a little, so he told him to go ahead. The man that walked in was as big as Beckett. Not fat, but tall and muscled. They hugged, and then Houston sat down on the couch across from him.

"Beckett told me about Allie losing her job today. Or I guess yesterday. I'd like to explain it to her if you think that will help her to understand." He said they'd both read the paper. "All the paper is telling people is what we wanted them to know. Yes, there were children hurt, but what they don't say is that they were our nephews."

"Are you having a fucking party out here?" Allie stood there with her sloppy T-shirt on and her very thin and see-through robe open. No shoes, no slippers, and certainly nothing under the shirt. That was very obvious by the way the light in the hall silhouetted her body from behind. Allen told her to go change; they had to talk. "Sure. Why the fuck not? I wasn't sleeping anyway. There's a fucking party going on out here. Do you need me to whip up some snacks while I'm at it? I have a nice vial of arsenic someplace I can sprinkle over the top of some popcorn."

She continued to mumble about noise and football as she made her way back to her room. Allen started to apologize to the men, but they were both smiling like they didn't have an ounce of sense. Allie was going to kill them both. He just knew it. Him too if she wasn't finished with her anger by the time they were both bleeding out on the floor.

Allen went into the kitchen to pop some popcorn. Her bringing it up made him hungry for it.

~*~

Beckett watched the hallway. It would be his luck that she decided to go back to bed and leave him hanging.

Smiling to himself, he couldn't believe his luck. His car breaking down right outside the house that his mate lived in. And she, according to her brother, was as mean as the other women. When she finally came down the hallway again, he stood up. So did his brother. She only stared at them before telling them to stop being a fucking jack in the box. Beckett was laughing when he sat back down.

"What the hell are you doing here? Do you have any idea what time it is? We both have lives that we're trying to get to in the morning." Allen explained to his sister who they were. "I don't care if they're strippers at this point. I just want you to tell me why we're having guests here, and that— Is that caramel popcorn?"

"I thought it might make you in a better mood." She told him good luck with that and took the bowl from him. "Allie, this is Beckett and Houston Robinson. They're here to talk to you about why you lost your job today."

She put the bowl down and looked so sad that Beckett wanted to comfort her. Instead, he handed her the bowl back and told her it wasn't that bad. She just stared at him, then looked at Houston before speaking.

"It doesn't matter how bad it is. I'm no longer employed. And that fucking sucks. I didn't know a thing about what was going on in the classrooms because they didn't hire me as a teacher. I work in the stupid lunchroom. Do you have any idea how many times you have to tell a kid that it's not poison we're feeding them, but a nutritious meal? Kids are odd. Also, I want to point out that I had nothing at all to do with the food that is

missing. That shit was going on long before I got there."
Houston asked her about the food missing. "Mostly, it's
things like ham and beef that comes up missing. No one
bothers with the tuna or the fish. But they're also taking
out long sleeves of napkins, as well as some of the chafing
dishes. I thought for sure they'd bring those back. But
this morning, or yesterday now, they were still missing."

"What do you know about the kids being hurt?" She
said she'd not been told anything other than that some
rich kids' parents were making a stink about some kids
being hurt on the playground. "It's a bit more than that.
One of the boys has broken ribs and a fractured arm, and
the other is bruised up badly as well. Someone actually
stitched up one of the kids and never notified us about
his injuries."

"It was the nurse, wasn't it?" Houston told her it was
her and the principal. "Figures. You said you weren't
notified. I'm assuming you're involved in this to your
neck. Not that it matters, I guess. If the nurse is in on it,
you can bet that the other teachers have signed off on
keeping their mouths shut about anything that happens
there."

"What do you mean?" Instead of answering his
brother, Allie got up and went to her room again. When
she returned, she had a file that had the name of the school
on it, as well as the logo emblazoned over it. When she
handed it to Houston, she looked at Beckett.

"You're here for a reason other than your stupid car
breaking down, aren't you?" He nodded. "Whatever it

is, I don't want anything to do with it. I'm sorry, but I've enough shit on my plate as it is, and I cannot balance another thing. You'll just have to do whatever it is elsewhere."

"You're my mate." She cursed, long and violently. Each word that wasn't a curse word was something to do with his anatomy. It wouldn't bode well for him if he was to get closer to her. Beckett was sure too that she would do just what she said she would if he were to push her. "If it makes you feel any better, I can help you out with some of your plate balancing."

"No, it doesn't." She turned to her brother. "You knew this when you told me to come out here and have a conversation with them. Any reason you didn't tell me? Or at least warn me of this?"

"I'm hurt badly enough, thanks." She snorted at him, and Beckett laughed. "He's odd like that, so you know. He laughs at the strangest things. Allie, just listen to them both for now. You can work out the rest later. This is important to a great many people."

"This is a nondisclosure contract that states you will never testify against your fellow workers, nor will you bring up any charges against them. Did you sign this?" She said she'd not gotten around to it. "Good for you. This might be just what we need to make sure they all serve jail time."

"I don't know why, in your addled mind, you'd think I'd testify against them. I need a job. Badly. I also need someplace to live. Snitching on them will blackball me for the rest of my life. I might as well become a flipping attorney for all the love I'll get from any place that I might apply to from now on." Houston asked her if she hated attorneys. "I don't know any. I do know they're not well-liked, and that right there will put me in with them in the friendly department. I can't afford this."

Houston looked at Beckett. When he nodded at his brother, he thought that telling her some things he'd be able to help her with would be a terrible idea. But it also might make it so they'd get this taken care of before more things befell her and her brother.

"I know you don't want to hear this right now, but you don't have to worry about money. Neither of you do." She snorted at him. "You do that very well, but it's the truth. Right now, I can put you in a position that you'd not ever have to worry about money again. That goes for your brother too."

"So, you're going to blackmail me into being your mate. That's a low blow, bringing my brother into this too." Beckett said she had a very suspicious mind, and that wasn't what he was saying at all. "Look. I'll help you with the kitchen shit. That's all I know for sure. But as far as being a mate to you, I'm sorry, but you know nothing about me that makes me feel like this would work. I'm sure you're a very nice man, but you've no idea what— I'm not the sort of person people want to date a second time. I'm mouthy, bitchy, and I don't beat around the bush. You'd better not either if you think any woman would want to be with you. You have no idea of the shit that I have in my life right now."

"You're not giving me anything that makes me think we're not perfectly matched." Beckett thought about his next statement. "I understand your frustration, Allie. I really do. However, you just flat out telling me that it won't work isn't something I can live with. What is it you think you're going to tell me, or I'll find out, that is going to make me walk away? And so you know, I'm not a man who gives up easily."

"I've killed a man." He knew it was more than that. Beckett also knew she was hoping she'd say just enough that he'd be out the door. Instead of moving, he asked her what he'd done to her to make her have to kill him. "Just like that. You know I didn't just kill him?"

"Yes. You're not stupid. You're also very straightforward. I doubt very much that you'd just murder someone without just cause. So, I ask you again, what did he do to you that made you have to kill him?" She looked at her brother, and he did as well. "Does she want you to tell me? I'm sure it's not as cut and dried as she says."

"It's not. She killed him because he was…taking advantage of her. Not to rape her, as she had thought at first. But he wanted to experiment on her. Flaying her skin off her arms to see her pain level was just one of the many things he had planned for her when he took her. Allie, being a redhead, has been the subject of many speculations on things like her being soulless, her pain level being high, as well as how much she needs in the way of pain medication when she's hurt. Things that are simply rumors. This man thought he'd prove to the world that it was a fact that redheads were special." Beckett asked him how she'd killed him. "With the knife he had stuck into her arm. She slit his throat from ear to ear. He was dead even before she was able to pull out the other things he'd put into her to test her."

Beckett looked at Allie. She wasn't looking at anyone now, her head bowed and her body stiff with what he thought was anger. Getting up, he moved closer to her on the couch and asked if she'd show him the scars. It wasn't until she pulled up her sleeve that he realized this had happened recently. There were still scabs on the wound at her bicep.

"This was recently." She told him about three months ago, but some of the wounds were taking longer to heal because they were so deep. "Are there other wounds? What else did he do to you, love?"

She leaned forward on the couch and tried to lift her shirt. What he saw there made him slightly ill. Allie had been beaten. From the looks of some of the scarring and wounds, he'd say it had happened over a period of several days. He asked her how long she'd been captured.

"Eight days. I was headed to the airport to go and see my brother. I was told that there would be a limo to take me to the airport. But once I was in the sucker, he took me to his lair. Or whatever he called his place. No one bothered looking for me because they'd thought I was with Allen. All the time I was being a science project for some dick." Without asking, Beckett leaned in and licked the worst of the wounds. The taste of infection hit his system, and he told her what he'd found. "I know that. It's hard for me to put anything on the ones back there. But I'll manage."

"My brothers are doctors." Beckett reached out to Thatcher since he knew that Dawson was on call and asked him to come to this house. He also told him that his mate had been beaten recently. He told him that he was bringing Rogen with him as they were in the car together. "Thatcher is coming to have a look at this. Didn't the hospital treat these wounds?"

"They wouldn't take me." She glanced at her brother when he told him why. "See? That's just one more thing I have stacked against me. I'm too broke to have insurance no matter what the laws say otherwise. Even the clinic that I went to yesterday told me that I'd have to wait on a background check before I could be seen by anyone."

Allie stood up, and so did he. She was taller than he'd thought she was. Putting his hand on her other wound, he told her she was a little feverish as well. He could see it in her eyes now that he was looking at her. When she swayed a little, he picked her up and held her in his arms. When she didn't argue, he knew she had been fighting this all evening, which he'd bet was making her weaker every minute.

By the time Thatcher and Rogen showed up, he'd taken Allie to the shower to try and cool her down. She was talking, babbling now about how she'd lost her job to little people. There was one point where she said that there were monsters, great giant ones, chasing her through the school. While he had no idea what she might have thought was chasing her, he did have to hold her tighter when she began fighting them off.

Beckett had a bloodied nose and a sore jaw when he was finally able to get her cooled off enough that Thatcher was satisfied. He gave her something for the pain, then set her up with an IV. Her temp spiked again, and Thatcher said she'd have to go to the clinic now. As Beckett carried her toward his truck, she looked up at him.

"Just let me die. I'm such a fuck up." He told her not to him she wasn't. "But you don't know what you're getting in me, Beck. What if I'm not any good in bed?"

"You will be perfect." She talked some more, and he had to hold her tightly as they made their way to the clinic. When they pulled into the parking lot, she was burning up again, her body shaking so hard that he was having a difficult time holding her still.

"Change her." They all looked at Allen when he spoke. He'd only just gotten the straps on her arms and legs so she'd not hurt herself or anyone else. "She's been ill for a week or more. She's been telling me she's getting better. Change her before she dies. Please. She's all I have in the world. Change her so she'll be all right."

Beckett looked at Thatcher, and he agreed. This was something he wasn't sure was a good idea. Thatcher told him that her organs would shut down before too much longer, and then she'd be too weak to make it either way. Letting his tiger take him, Beckett knew this was going to cause him all kinds of trouble. But she'd be alive, and that was all that mattered right now.

Jumping up on the bed she was strapped to, he was glad that Thatcher had shifted as well. Between the two of them, she'd change so much faster. The only thing that worried him at the moment, however, was what she was going to do to him when she found out. Again, he told himself, she'd be alive, and that was all that mattered. He hoped that he was right. Christ, she was going to be pissed off.

Chapter 3

Allen watched his sister rest. He'd been given a room next to hers, and that was making it easier for him to go and see her. Allie had been out for four days now, and he was beginning to worry about her. They all told him that she had been really sick to begin with, and that's what was making her sleep so long. He wanted her to wake up so that she could curse him out. He had no doubt that it would be high on her list of things to do.

The knock at the door warned him that he was going to have company. It was Beckett.

"Any changes?" He told him that she glared at him a little bit ago but hadn't spoken. "Yeah, I'm thinking we'll be lucky if that's all she does to us." They both laughed.

"I've been meaning to ask you about this place we're staying in. I'm assuming it's your home." He said that it was when he was home. "Your dad told me that you're very hush hush about what you do for a living. I'm assuming it's legal."

"It is. Why would you assume otherwise? Just curious. I mean, you have met my mom. Does she strike you as someone that would allow her child to be a criminal?" Allen laughed with the other man. "It's not so much that I'm hush hush about it, but I'm just working hard at not making a name for myself. I go into businesses that are failing and work there for a few weeks. Sometimes it takes less time, but I find out where they're lacking in the way things are working. Mostly it's human error that is causing the deficiency, but not always. They pay well, but I also get a percentage of what they make in viable profit the first year after I've been there, and they've done what I suggested. If it was out there who I was, I doubt very much I could blend in the way I do."

"You wouldn't blend into a tree if you were dressed all in bark." They both looked at Allie when she spoke. "Why do I have a feeling I'm not in Kansas anymore?"

"You're in Beckett's home. This was the best place to bring you to recuperate after you decided not to tell anyone you were sick. How are you feeling, sis?" Allie sat up, then laid back down with her eyes closed. "You look a great deal better than you did four days ago."

"Four days? No wonder I feel weird. Can I have a glass of water? I feel like I have cotton in my mouth." Beckett got her a glass of the water that had been brought up here every couple of hours. He helped her drink from the glass he'd poured her, as she still looked slightly out of it. When she seemed to have enough, Beckett sat down again. "I know this is your house and all, but I'd like to talk to my brother for a minute. Without you."

"Your meanness is showing again." Allie stuck her tongue out at Beckett as he made his way to the door. "If you feel like something to eat in a little while, I'll bring it up. Thatcher said soup to start with, then more if you keep that down. I'll see you later, Allen."

As soon as he was out the door, Allie sat up in the bed. She did look better today. Her hair was, of course, a mess, but she wasn't as pale as death anymore. Getting up, Allen handed her a brush that had been in the bathroom, as well as a small mirror. Allie worked on the tangles while he told her about some of the things going on.

"The kitchen staff has been arrested. There was more going on there than just a few missing pans and food. Apparently, they were also taking the money at the end of the day and splitting it between them. I had a feeling from what Rogen told me that you wouldn't have been a part of it even if you wanted. They were a group that shared the same secret as to how it was being done."

"Why am I here instead of a hospital? I can remember bits and pieces of when I passed out, but not too much of it makes any sense." He told her what he knew, skipping over the part where she'd been changed. "I didn't tell you I was sick because I knew you had enough on your mind. I really didn't know I was that sick. But it was almost as soon as he touched me, I felt like the world was coming down on my head, and he was the only one that could keep me from getting badly hurt. That's weird, isn't it?"

"Not if you think about the fact that he's your mate. I mean, that's what is supposed to happen, right?" She said she didn't want him as a mate. "I have something to tell you, Allie. Well, two things. You're not going to like either one of them. I had them change you into a tiger in order to save your life."

"I'm sorry, what did you do?" He repeated what he'd said to her. "No, you did not take it upon yourself to have some overgrown cat change me into something that I can't change back. Allen, why would you do that?"

"To save your life. He was all there was between you and death. I told him to do it. No matter what he tells you, it was all on me." She asked him if Beckett had argued much at the idea. "Yes. Quite a bit, as a matter of fact. It wasn't until you coded that he decided I was correct. And I need you in my life as much as you need me, Allie. The thought of going on without you was too much to care about how mad you'd be when you woke up."

She looked out the window that showed the pool off to its best advantage. Not only was there a pool in Beckett's back yard, but there was a hot tub, as well as a screened-in area that Allen had been spending a lot of time in.

"You said there were two things." He asked her what she meant. "You told me you have two things to tell me. I'm assuming you didn't mean the arrests as one of them."

"No. That's not the other thing. You weren't human. Even before he changed you into a tiger, you were never human before that. Not wholly anyway. Thatcher helped with your change, and he told me later that you'd not been born as a vampire, but he thinks that since the guy who took you was one, he might well have bitten you a few times when you were out. Holland wasn't a pure vampire either, or you would have been able to heal on your own from what you got from him." She looked at him then. There was shock there, but he had a feeling she was thinking too. "You did tell me that Holland disappeared after you cut him. He didn't escape like we thought, but simply ceased to be."

"The police still believe I made all that up. That I'd never been taken and that there was no one in that place with me. They'll not believe me anymore now that we know what he was, will they?" Allen didn't have an answer for her, so he said nothing. "What happens to me now, Allen? I mean, surely Beckett isn't going to want a half breed around now that he knows. A vampire is something that very few people even believe in."

"He does. His family does as well. Rogen, she's Thatcher's wife, has a way of getting in and out of all kinds of programs and locked files. She said she was going to fix it so it would be like it never occurred. According to your records anyway." She asked him what good that would do. "It wouldn't come up when someone did a background check, for one thing. Also, someone's put money in our accounts. Several checks were going to bounce. I asked and was told that there wasn't any reason for that to happen. Not while you were laid low."

"I don't know how I feel about that either." Allen told her to just be calm about it. That they were trying their best to make things less stressful for the two of them. "What about you? I mean, someone had to notice that you're limping around too."

"They have. I've been given some information about my injury that makes me believe it was more than just an accident. That the reason the service hasn't acknowledged what happened to me is because they're working hard on sweeping it under the rug, so no one finds out. I was shot by friendly fire, Allie. I didn't know that before." Allie asked him what happened now. "I get to get my leg fixed. They'll also be responsible for me getting my checks that had been held back. I had no idea that I should have still been getting a check when I was discharged. Did you?"

"No. But if you remember, I did mention that." He said that he told Rogen that too. "And I bet she ignored it like your commanding officer did."

"Actually, she told me that if I would listen to you more rather than thinking of you like my little sister, I might well have been further along in my recovery. They're all excited to meet you. Beckett said I could tell you some things about his family if you want to know." Allie asked if they were all huge like the two that she'd met. "Yes. There are six of them. Boys, their parents call them, of the Robinson family. Three of them are married now, not including you and Beckett. They're really nice people. I've gotten to have a meal with them every night since we've been brought here."

"You make it sound like it's a done deal between Beckett and I. It's not, Allen. Even you can see that our lives aren't quite like those of the people who live here. We're poor." He nodded and smiled at her. "You know how much I hate when you look at me like that. What is it you have up your sleeve that you think I need to know about?"

"Two days ago, your name was added to everything Beckett has. I have a car to use should I need to get around. Not a used one, but a brand new one. Like the one you have." She told him she didn't have a car. "You do now. And while I know you're smart enough to realize when a good thing is right in your lap, I don't want to have to remind you that before you met Beckett, we were not only not going to be able to live in the house we were in, but the town either. Allie, we were so close to the edge of losing everything, and some things that we didn't have, that it's a small wonder there was any food in the house."

"I don't like this." He said he didn't blame her one bit. She looked out the window again, and he didn't say anything, waiting until she turned back to him. But she didn't. Speaking to him without looking at him, she asked him to leave her alone for a little while. "I just need to think. It's too much. All at once, this is too much for me. I need to be able to sort things out on my own for a little while."

"All right. But I'll be back later, all right?" She nodded, and he saw the tear roll down her cheek. Before he could tell her not to cry, she told him she was all right and that she needed some time to herself. "I love you, Allie. Very much so. I only did what I thought was best to keep you alive. You understand that, don't you?"

"I do." The smile she gave him when she turned didn't reach her tear-filled eyes. "I'm going to be all right like you said. When you come back, I'll be able to talk to you about what has happened. Right now, I just need to think."

He left her then, using the cane that he'd been given in physical therapy. Allen had forgotten to tell her about that. But they had time. They had lots of time to talk now that she was better.

Allen found Beckett in his office on the telephone. Before he could walk out of the office again, Beckett waved him in. After he was seated, he looked around the big place. The man must have every book ever printed in this room alone. Beckett grinned at him when he was able to get off the phone.

"I have pissed off the last place I worked for. They thought I was going to tell them there was nothing to do but close the building down. I don't know why they'd be eager to do that, but I've told them I won't sign off on that sort of thing. How is she? As mad as we thought she'd be about being here?" Allen told him that he'd told her about being a tiger and how he'd put money in their accounts. "Is she gunning for me?"

"No. She told me she just wanted to think things over. That it was just a lot of things at once. I don't know, but

I think she's really upset." Beckett told him she was — he could feel it. "Should I go back up there and sit with her?"

"I'd not. If she asked for the time to think, she more than likely needs it. I know she's been thrown a curveball in all this." Allen told him that they all had. "Yes, I guess we have. By the way, Rogen said she might have a job for you. Something you can do while you're healing. I don't know what it might be, but if she says you can do it, then you can believe you'll be able to. She also wants to talk to you about your injury."

"I'll tell her whatever she wants to know." Beckett nodded and said she'd be over to get him soon. "I wish they'd let me drive wherever they want me. It seems like a lot of wasted time in everyone carting me around."

"Rogen likes to pick people up so that she can grill them while she takes them places. Don't tell her I said that. She's been really cranky since she's been in her last few weeks of pregnancy. My brother, Thatcher, has been hanging out here a little more to make sure he doesn't stress her out too much. Rogen and my other sisters, they're what you might not ever think of as gentle women."

"No, I don't think I would." Allen laughed. "I've met them all now, and they scare the crap out of me. One on one, they're not too bad — I can handle that. But with all three of them together, it's scary as fuck."

"Wait until your sister joins them." Allen thought about that for about two seconds before he shivered.

"Yes, exactly what I was thinking too."

Rogen showed up about five minutes later. Before she wanted to leave, however, she wanted to go up and introduce herself to Allie. Both he and Beckett told her she should wait, but she climbed the stairs anyway. He was almost afraid to see the room after this meeting. The two of them together were going to be as volatile as a match to gasoline.

~*~

Allie knew who the woman was the second she came into the room. She'd been there briefly when Allie had fallen ill, but she knew a ball-buster when she saw one. Asking her what she wanted didn't help with her mood any more than it did Allie's. But when Rogen sat down in the chair next to her, she decided that she could explain herself instead of Allie asking her questions.

"I'm glad to see you up and around. Did they tell you that you've been changed into a tiger yet?" She glared at the woman. "I see they did. Oh well, I'm sure there are a couple of things that they didn't mention. I was wondering what you wanted to do with the rest of your life."

"Live. What do you want to do with the rest of your life? Or is it all sewn together nicely for you now?" Rogen didn't seem to know what to say about that. "I have a home that I've not been in other than this room. Money in my account so I'd not bounce checks. I'm out of a job, no longer human, and at one point, I was part vampire. Now I'm fully tiger. Did I miss anything?"

"You're snarky." Allie told her that she was as well. "True, but I've always been that way. Usually, you're thought of as too nice and gullible for anyone to want to be around. Not what I would categorize you as right now."

"Goody for you. What do you want, Rogen? I have things that I have to work out, and you here being the bitch that you are isn't helping me get a grip on shit." Rogen laughed. "Of course, you'd find that funny. Why are you here? Did I miss one of the perks that the great Robinsons gave to me when they changed me into this without permission?"

"Would you rather be dead?" Allie told her that she would, actually. "You don't mean that. You're just saying that so that you can shock me."

Allie got up and went to the bed she'd been in. Pulling out the gun she'd found in this room when she'd been looking for something to wear, she put it to her head. The two of them watched each other for several minutes until Rogen stood up.

"There is a man downstairs that is in love with you. Too much for you right now? Too fucking bad. If you kill yourself over what was done to save your life, then he will die right along with you. Not because he'll end his life too, but he'll have to be put down because you're dead. Also, you might really want to think this over before you pull that trigger. What do you think this will do to Allen? He seems to like you for some reason. Right now, all I see is a lazy bitch trying to end her life because someone loved her enough to want her to be around." Rogen went to the door and opened it. "The safety is on that gun. I didn't want you to miss the opportunity to end your life because the gun didn't work, and you got to have second thoughts."

The door closed quietly behind her, and Allie burst into tears. Sitting on the floor with the gun still in her hands, she wondered if her life would ever be her own. It didn't seem like it from where she was sitting. Getting up, she decided that she might as well figure shit out. Killing herself now would make it so that Rogen won. Won what, she didn't know, but Allie knew the other woman would feel like she'd taken gold if she were to go through with killing herself.

She decided it was time to tell them something. Reaching out to Beckett, she thought of the others too. But for now, Beckett needed to understand what she had gone through. Not enough, she supposed, to kill herself over. But she'd been—

When I was dropped off at the home, I didn't have any kind of identification on me—nothing to tell them why I'd been left there. No name. I was a newborn. They knew that. Whoever had me had taken me directly to the home without even the benefit of cleaning me up, I was told. She leaned back against the bed to continue. *I didn't have anything that belonged to me. Not even my name. Fifty-two other children before me had the same name. I was called fifty-three for the entire time I was at the home. After a little bit, I started referring to myself as Grace. I have no idea why that was the name I wanted. But no one would play along with me. Then I was adopted.*

She thought about the day she'd found out that Allen was going to leave her. He'd been her protector when the other kids needed someone to beat on or to blame something they'd done on. Crashing into the meeting, she'd climbed up in his arms and begged him not to leave her. The Langleys thought she was adorable and had taken her too.

I'd been given the chance, the Langleys told me, to choose the color of my room. I didn't have any idea what that might involve, but I told them they could call me Grace. After the laughter died down, they said I'd be Allie. Allen and Allie, their children. I think it should be pointed out that their names were Paul and Paula. Allen had his name already. So I was now Allie Langley. Beckett asked her if she had a middle name. *No. I don't know why, but I was only adopted as Allie. Which I have to admit, was difficult to be called. Everyone I had to deal with thought it was short for something. I got into a lot of fights at school over it. Do you know when Allen will be back from the job you guys have him on? He came up long enough to say goodbye.*

Not for some time yet. What else do you remember from being with the Langleys? Anything I should know about? She told him she didn't think so but did think of the fights she'd get into at school about her stupid name.

She laughed when she thought of some of the scraps she'd gotten into at school. It wasn't until she was ten that she realized fighting got her nowhere but in trouble. Not just at home, but at school as well.

I dreamt of being something important. When you're ten, you think that anything you do is important, I suppose. But I didn't want to be a teacher. I know that everyone thinks that was my dream job — it wasn't. I was settling, in a way. Even if all I could do was teach, I was going to be the best teacher in the world. Again, I was ten at the time. She thought of the conversations that had prompted her to settle. *The Langleys were good to me. They loved me, showed me right from wrong. They were huggers too, so I came to depend on that, I guess you could say. But the one thing that they lacked and I needed was the ability to be encouraging. Not to pave the way for me, but just to tell me to go for it. Nothing that I wanted to do, not even to be a gardener, which is something that I had dreamed of, was anything they thought I would succeed at. Not only that, but they told me that with my looks, I'd be better off just settling down with a husband and having children for him. And to hope that none of them would be born as a redhead.*

What a horrible thing to say to someone. Allie didn't know who had spoken, their voices were different in her head, but she did defend the Langleys to the voice. *Yes, well, I can see where you might be grateful for having a good home. But to say something like that to a child is deplorable.*

The fear of having a child that had red hair was another reason I settled on teaching. I could have as many children around me as I wanted and never have to have the stress of having someone that looked like me. That was nailed home to me when I was kidnapped one afternoon and experimented on because of my hair color. Allie reached for a tissue that was on the side table. The tears were blinding her; she was crying so hard. *I'd had a front-row seat to knowing what people thought of when they saw a redheaded person. Okay, I'm not naïve enough to think that everyone thinks like my stepparents or the man who had taken me felt. But I did feel as if I lost something else that I had no control over.*

I'm coming up, Allie.

She didn't say anything to Beckett. She had it in her head that he was going to tell her she was too loaded down with issues. That he'd not thought of her being someone with red hair and what it would do to one of his children. When he entered the room, she stayed where she was and looked at him. His smile, brilliant with happiness, was exactly what she needed.

Beckett helped her up from the floor and held her tightly against his body. He didn't speak — what could he say? she thought. But when he lifted her chin up so that they could look at each other, Allie held her breath.

"I love you. So very much." The burst of acceptance came out as a giggle. "Christ, you're amazing. And I am forever sorry for changing you. Bringing you here. These are the other things you didn't mention that were out of your control. No wonder you were upset. I think I would have been as well."

"I'm just whiny." He said she was sharing her life with them. "I hadn't any idea I was sharing with the others. But then I thought they might as well understand too. I think I pissed off Rogen. I'll have to keep looking over my shoulder for a hitman until I can make this right."

"She won't kill you. She'd hire someone else to do it. More than likely, it will be some drone loaded up with some kind of killer bullet." Allie stared at him. "I'm not joking about the drone, but she won't hurt you. When she told me she pissed you off enough for you to put a gun to your head, I didn't know what to say. But she did feel really bad about it."

"Is all of your family like her?" He said just the women. "I see. So the men, they're what? Lazy bums? Men who allow their wives to—"

"I think you misunderstood. We don't *allow* our wives to do anything. They want to do it, they do it. None of us argue." He laughed. "Do you think we're stupid enough to tangle with them? Any one of them could call down a world of hurt on us that would last forever. No, we don't even consider thinking that we could allow them to do anything. I won't you either."

"Thank you for that. I do want to try things. I might well fail at everything I do, but I want to have the ability to at least say that I failed, not that I'd quit." She laid her head on his chest. "I'm sorry. I'm so very sorry for what I did. Not just to you, but your family as well. I was being a bitch."

When he didn't agree or disagree, she was ready to pop him in the nose. But he was looking out the window, and she started to turn to see what had grabbed his attention. Before she could go to the window, he told her to move slowly and not to make any noise. Through the open window, she could hear grunts and squeals.

"They're baby bears. Look at them. They're just little guys." He said they were killer babies if they tried to pet them. "Oh Beck, they're amazing. I see mamma bear now. Will they get into the pool?"

They did. One at a time, they slid into the large pool. Mamma bear sat on the edge, seemingly telling them to behave when they started tossing water at her. Watching them was like having her faith renewed in life. A new beginning, Allie thought.

Turning to Beck, she realized he was watching her. As he took a step toward her, she wanted to feel his arms around her. His mouth on hers. So when he leaned down to kiss her, Allie gave him everything she had in the kiss. And it wasn't nearly enough. Allie wondered briefly if it would ever be enough coming from this man.

Chapter 4

The books that Tru handed over to Allie were still sitting on the desk where she'd put them. Not wanting to dress the girl down on doing what she told her to do, Tru let out a long breath and went to find her. Allie wanted to help, but this was the second time she'd come here to talk to her, and she was gone. Finding her in the dining room, she watched her for a couple of seconds before she realized what she was doing. Allie turned and looked at her.

"I'm sorry." Tru nodded, looking at the artwork that was now on the dining room table. "I read the books. I know you didn't think I was doing it—Rogen told me—but I did. When she handed me this file on the last robbery, I needed a visual to make it work in my head."

"It's the bakery." Allie showed her what she'd been using for each item that had been listed on the inventory sheet. "The pepper shaker, what is that representing?"

"The robber. I know he went there in the middle of

the night, he said, because he'd seen the safe earlier in the day and the combo when it had been opened. But it just doesn't work out as he is saying it went down." There were paper towel walls around the office. The door had been made from another paper towel. Tru had seen the drawing of the place, but this, even to her, was much more visible. "See? The door to the office opens to the back of the shop. The only way he could have seen it was if he'd been coming from the rear."

"I didn't realize the door was at that angle. Where did you see this?" Allie showed her how the store's map was wrong according to the report that the manager had verbally given her. "We'll have to go and see which way it is. I mean, this was given to me, and I've not been able to get around to looking over the paperwork."

"I did. I went there before I started playing with this. You can see the office is there, but there isn't a window — again, something he mentioned too." Tru was very impressed. She also wondered if Allie had any idea how brilliantly she was doing this. "I tried even making him come into the rear of the shop, but there isn't a window to break to get in. Besides, the walk-in is most of the back of the shop anyway. Too many layers, I'd think, to just pop through."

Tru asked Rogen and Anna to come into the dining room. They'd been working in the house the last few days so that the babies could see them. Tru had Allie explain what she'd come up with.

"So you're thinking he had help from someone on

the inside rather than just coming in and breaking the glass to get to the safe." Allie looked embarrassed when Anna spoke to her, and she asked her what she thought then. "You have an idea of how this happened. We can read your mind, but I'd rather you just tell us what you came up with. Come on, Allie. We're all working together here. Get your shit together."

"There was no robbery." That wasn't what any of them expected. "There was money taken, but not by anyone but the store manager. If you'll remember from the file, it said that she was getting sick of this happening to her. So, I hope you don't mind, but I looked back over the records of the place. The newspaper put it on the front page every time it happened. It's usually before a holiday that the place is taken."

Allie handed her notes to her, and she glanced at them before handing them off to Rogen. When Allie started to take the model apart, Rogen stopped her. After going over each of the scenarios again, they all agreed that it had to be an inside job.

"I'm going to get you a 3-D printer. And a bunch of blocks." Tru walked around the table and could see other items Allie had used as parts of the shop. "Also, I'd think you could use some little furniture. A car or two. This is amazing. And the fact that you were able to go there firsthand and see what you need has impressed the hell out of me."

"I was letting the stuff you had me read settle in my head and this sort of popped in there. And I don't know what I'd do with a printer. I've never used one of those kind before." The more Tru walked around the thing, the more she could see how much time and effort Allie had taken with this. Tru asked her how long it had taken her. "Not very long. It was finding things that I could use for the shop that took the most time. The paper towels were easier. I could cut them down to the size I needed."

"We'll have someone train you on the printer. It'll be easy once you have that down." Anna was standing where the entrance of the shop was—there was toilet paper there to represent the street. "Christ, you even drew little cars here so we'd know this was the front of the place. I'm so excited to see how you can make this work for other crime scenes."

"Me too." Rogen moved around the table too, but she was bulky right now with her baby showing so much. "I have two other files like this one. Where whatever went down isn't adding up. Like Tru said, I believe that this will cut down on a lot of going there and coming back to try and work out the details. This is your job from now on if you want it. This is going to save us all a lot of time, Allie. Thanks so much."

"I was just trying to get it straight in my head." Rogen told her she'd done that and more. "You don't have to give me a job, guys. I was just sort of bored and needed something to occupy my mind while the things in the book settled around me. I don't mind doing this for you, but you don't have to pay me for having some fun."

"You took what, an hour to make this thing?" Allie

told Tru yes, about that. "We've had this sitting in a file for a couple of weeks to see what sort of progress we could make on it. You not only figured it out by playing around, as you called it, but I believe you're right. It's done from the inside. If you only did this for us a few times a month, you'd be saving us a great deal of time and resources. You're hired. I'm standing here thinking of all the shit you could do once you set your mind to it."

Pride. Tru knew only too well how good it could feel to have someone be prideful of your job. She thought perhaps Allie hadn't gotten any of that growing up. To think that they told her basically not to breed. Tru hoped that every one of her children were little redheaded monsters. It would be awesome for both her and Beckett.

Rogen left them for a few minutes as she and Anna went over the project with Allie. Not to have her explain how she'd done it, but to get the details on how she'd come up with the conclusion. Tru realized a couple of things about Allie that she liked.

One, she didn't chatter or need to fill in silence when it wasn't necessary. She thought about what she was going to say, then said it. There wasn't any "I think" or "I believe" either. Allie knew what she'd figured out and wasn't backing off when questioned about it.

The second thing she realized was that Allie did need to have her information settle in her mind. Tru took a quick peek into her head and was amazed to feel her putting things in her mind in order. Taking information that she could use and sliding it into something to remember it by. Tru would bet anything that if someone could look into her mind and what she was doing, it would look like filing cabinets with names on the drawers for her to be able to retrieve the information quickly. It was what she did when she read something she needed to blend in with. File after file of information.

Rogen joined them again a few minutes later. "I'm having someone come out in the morning to build you a space to use. I don't know that you'll need a huge space, but you will need room to put out diagrams and such. Also, they're going to send over some of the things we talked about." She grinned at them. "You should have heard the man when I told him we needed blocks that could be used for a housing project. He was excited as hell to get them for us—also people. I didn't know how many you'd need, but he had a good idea in saying he'd fix them so that you could add things to them. Such as bullet holes and knife wounds."

"You're serious about this." Rogen told Allie she was seldom not serious about her work. "What are you going to do with all this stuff if it turns out this is a one-time deal with me? For all you know, I could have spent the bank on this project and won't know how to do it the next time."

"Do you believe this was a one time shot? Tell me now if you do. Not that I'll believe you if you tell me it was. You have a mind that works on a level that frankly makes me jealous. You can take a crime scene and make it into something that is not only easier to see, but you've done it in a way that makes me think you're perfect at seeing outside the box." Allie admitted that she did this kind of thing all the time when she wanted to move her furniture around. "Great. Once you get the proper equipment, you'll be able to make things to scale or as close to it as you can. Crime scenes will be something that will get the most use of this. In that, you'll be able to put in just what was at the crime scene and look at it from not only every angle but from overhead. That alone, to me, sounds like a good thing to have. No more tromping through a field or forest either. You'd have it all right here so that we can move it and use it over and over as more information comes to light. You have to do this for us, Allie. This is absolutely the next step in solving the most heinous of crimes."

"I'll do it." Tru was glad. She didn't want to have to bully her into helping them. Even with the ways that Rogen said they'd use it, Tru could see even more uses.

Like when she had to get in and out of a place. In her job, she'd sometimes have to wing it and make adjustments to things that hadn't translated well to specs. Doorways and windows would help her in adjusting her travel through someone's home or office building. This would also make it so she'd be able to hide better if it all went to shit.

Allie was given the other files, and Tru watched her. It wasn't distracting for her, she told her. Tuning her out when she moved was easy for Allie. Using the same pieces that she'd gathered up, Tru laughed way harder than she should have when Allie went into the yard to get some small branches and twigs. Christ, this was going to be epic for all of them.

This file dealt with an outside shooting. Hills were made of rolled balls of paper towels. Small stones were around the "trees" to hold them upright. Allie even took copier paper and drew a little gun, as well as a rifle that had been found at the crime scene. Tru reached out to Rogen and told her that Allie would need an entire set of small guns and weapons.

I was thinking about that. Perhaps she'd be able to make them with the printer. I mean, any modifications that have been made to them as well. Rogen laughed. *Who would have thought that our little Allie would have a hidden talent like this? My mind is buzzing with the things she'll be able to help us with. Even setting up a building with her knowledge will be good for getting things in the right place the first time.*

Tomorrow, when this shit starts to show up, someone is going to have to be with her. Her poor little head will explode when she sees what you've ordered. I'm sure you went all out and got her everything she might ever need. Rogen said she didn't want her to be in the middle of a project and need something important. *Yes, you and I know that's how it will work, but she's going to think you went way overboard. I think for a few days, we're going to have to walk her through working for us. We might also want to bring her up to date on what it is we're doing here.*

Shit, I never thought of that. I wonder why she thinks we're doing this. Tru told her what she'd seen in her mind.

Attorney? I guess that makes sense. But when she hears that we kill people that need to be dead, I'm sure she's going to react badly. It's not something we put out there for even the family. They know, of course, but we started out this way. She's new to all of this.

I'm thinking she's not only going to be cool about all this, but I have a feeling she's not as timid as she's putting on. Once cornered, I'm betting she can fight better than any of us. Do you know if she uses a weapon? Rogen told her what had transpired in the bedroom. *Sure, she can hold it to her head, but can she kill someone who isn't trying to kill her first? That would be important if it ever came out what she can do. I'm thinking that if someone knew how well she can think like this, there will be hell to be paid.*

I don't think we should tell her that. Tru disagreed but said she'd wait until it became necessary. *All right. How is she doing with that file?*

She's done. Christ. I even know how it happened just by looking at it from this view. You have to come and see this. Hell, have everyone come and see this. With the right equipment and a worksheet, she'll be able to tell how we were conceived. Allie is going to be my go-to person when I'm stuck with what happened at a crime scene.

~*~

Beckett stretched out on the couch and closed his eyes. Today had been a killer of a day, and he just wanted to have some quiet time. He knew as soon as he heard the front door open and close that he was going to be shit out of luck. When he saw who was there, he smiled at Allie.

She was a distraction he could love.

"I'm in here," he called out to her when she yelled his name. "I just got home a few minutes ago, and I was going to catch a nap before supper. How was your first day of working with the others?"

She kicked off her shoes in the closet before coming into the living room. "Do you think they'd humor me at something I did?" He didn't know what she was talking about, but he did have an answer for her. "I didn't think so either. Apparently, they think they've found my dream job. It's really fun, so I'm having a difficult time thinking of it as work. They're having me make up models of crime scenes. Rogen ordered all kinds of tools for me to use when working with them. Also, and I find this a little hard to believe, they're buying a building that I can work from so that I can spread out. Can you rub my shoulders, please? I have a pulled place there."

She sat down on the couch when he sat up. "I take it that you're going to be working full time with them. I have to say, I think it's wonderful to have you here all the time. Which building are they thinking about?" She told him one of the larger buildings on the main drag through town. "I know those buildings. Any one of them will be good for working from. What is it you'll be doing with them?"

As she described what she'd done today and how it had helped, he knew for a fact that it hadn't been a humor job. They had been bitching about the bakery robbery for two weeks now and had been no closer to finding the person who had supposedly robbed the place.

"As it turned out, she'd been the one who had been robbing the place each time it had been done. Figuring out that she'd been using the money for family functions really pissed off her bosses. She'd ask for a few days to a week off after each time to settle her nerves. She was just going on vacation or something when the place was looked over for flaws." She sighed when he hit a sore spot, she told him. "I have to be trained on a 3-D printer too. Have you ever worked with one? Oh, that's perfect right there." He told her that he had, but he'd not been all that successful at it. "I wonder what will happen if I can't make it work either."

"I don't see you having issues with it. You can draw better than me, and that is where I messed up. Did you know you're bruised right here? It must have been recent, or you would have healed by now." Beckett loved how they could keep up conversations with each other and have other things to say as well. "It's fading, so it's nothing to worry about now."

She leaned back on his chest when he'd finished helping her out with her neck. It sounded like she'd had a good day. So when he was asked about his day, he almost didn't tell her.

"It started out well enough. I was supposed to look over some of the books for a company that makes salad dressings—all sorts. Before I even went to the place, I bought a few of their brand and decided I didn't care for it. Mom said she'd not cared for it either when she saw them in the fridge." When he told her the brand, she said that she hadn't cared for them either. "So I try and go in with an open mind. Once I was there, I saw a lot of health code violations right off the bat."

"Is that something you do as well? See if they're going to pass inspections?" Beckett told her not usually. "I would think that would be something someone would need to deal with right away. Yuck. Don't tell me what they were. I don't want to know."

"I wish I hadn't either. Anyway, I reached out to Thatcher and my dad—they used to have something to do with that sort of thing. I let them know what I was looking at and where I was. Both of them showed up on the pretense of having lunch with me. But as soon as they were in the door, the entire scam fell apart." He laughed a little. "Dad was appalled by what he'd seen. Thatcher gagged like fifty times when he saw it."

"Don't. Just move on to the part where the health department closed them down." He laughed all the harder. "They did, right? I'd hate to have to start a protest of the place. I will, too, if they make one more bottle of that nasty shit."

"Not only did they shut them down, but—" He was laughing too hard to catch his breath now. "Thatcher got sick, right there on the floor, while the inspector was pulling things away from the wall. Christ. Dad, he was patting my brother on the back, gagging too. It was, now that I'm not there, one of the funniest things I've ever seen. Employees were trying to clean up the puke, slipping and sliding all over the place. The inspector was ill too and had run to the bathroom three times before the police showed up. Oh, Allie, you've turned my shitty day into something I can laugh at now. Thank you, love."

"You're very welcome." She laughed with him when he described how green Thatcher had gotten. He told her how he'd had to go and shift to get the scent out of his nose. "I can almost see him doing that too. He's so stodgy. I'd not equate him with someone that would get sick when there is puking going on."

"He's always been like that. If one of us was sick, we'd never call on him. He would be joining us. Mom can just hear it, and it has her sick too." He pulled her over and sat her on his lap. He'd been thinking about her all day. "I wanted to tell you something. It's really important. But it's also something that was done behind your back. I didn't, but Rogen and the others did. They know who the vampire was that kidnapped you and hurt you. He's dead, as you well know."

"They felt I needed to know, right?" Beckett told her it was important that she knew, in the event, one of their children was a vampire. "I didn't think that would even be possible. Not with me being changed into a tiger."

"I don't know a great deal about it either, but I did get to talk to Dad about it. He said that the chances were slim, but something that we'd need to be prepared for. Not that I'd have any trouble with it, but they didn't know how you'd feel." She said if it were her child, she'd not care either. "I thought that was what you'd say. His

original name was Hampton. We're not sure if it was his
first or last name, or just the one he went by. He was born
in the late seventeenth century and had been alone for
most of that time."

"If you're going to tell me that's what made him
crazy, I think I got that." He said that was some of it, but
not all. "Did a redhead do something to him?"

"Yes. His wife, not his mate, had stepped out on
him. Then she'd turned him in as a night creature. The
police had tried to catch up with him, but he was just too
slick and fast for them. It turned out that she, Lily was
her name, had turned in his kiss too. There was a great
deal of money to be had for doing something like that."
Allie asked if they'd had children together. "Yes. Two.
But neither of them survived. It was thought that they'd
been taken by some humans and killed. However, now
they're thinking Lily herself killed them."

"Hampton. He kept telling me over and over that I
was going to be his greatest catch. That years of research
would proclaim him as a genius. I just thought he was
loony. Until he started cutting on me." Beckett felt her
tension and how she seemed to shake it off as quickly as
it had come over her. "No one would believe me when I
told them what had happened. I told your family just the
one time, and they figured out everything. I didn't want
to like them, I will tell you that, but I do, each of them.
They're harsh at times, the women, but I'm learning to
stand up to them if something isn't right."

"Did they tell you what they do? And who they do

it for?" Beckett didn't think they had, and he was right. "They each — and you would be considered a part of what they do—they're different parts of the whole that kills people that are fucking with the country. When we first met Rogen, she'd been hurt badly, saving a family. While we were trying to figure out where to put her while she healed, all kinds of government agencies came around to see how we'd measured up to what she would need in a cover."

Allie didn't say anything for a few minutes, but he could almost feel her mind working. When she turned to him, he could see that it only just occurred to her what he was saying. When she got up to pace, he waited until she had gone over everything in her head before she spoke.

"I thought they were attorneys or something that would work with them. Because of the way they wanted me to do the crime scenes so they could have the person arrested or something like that." He said that they more than likely did. "Let me think for a moment. Tru, she's the hitman or something like that. A cleanup person. The books she gave me were on things like going into a house and coming out with whatever they'd been sent in for. Anna is…she's a computer whiz. Not like Rogen is, but someone that can break into them and get what she wants out of them. Rogen, like I said, is the one that finds the person. Perhaps even tags them when the hit is called."

"You nailed them all." He grinned at her. "You only spent the day with them, and you pegged them perfectly.

What gave them away?"

"The way that Rogen, while sort of bossy, is never as secure in what she's doing unless she's sitting in front of a computer. She tries very hard to hide it, but it's a giveaway when she's right about something. Like she's surprised that she was. Let me see. Anna is a little harder to tell. She's street smart and rough around the edges. Hard, I think she'd be called. So is Tru, but she doesn't give two shits what you feel about her. Not even if you were to insult her to her face." She grinned at him. "I could be wrong about those traits. However, I do like them. They're mean when they mean well. They show affection like a schoolyard romance by hitting you. And when they love you, respect you, they rain it down on your head like it's a snowstorm in the mountains."

"I love you."

Allie looked at him with a strange look on her face. Beckett didn't know what she was thinking. Before he could ask her, however, she spoke.

"And I love you, Beck. I think I have for a while now. Even before I met you, I believe I was in love with the love you'd give me. You are the man I've dreamed of having in my life. Even before I knew I needed someone to love me, an image of you was right there, waiting and keeping me focused. Today when I saw your dad with your mom, all I could think about was how you were so much like him. Soft when you needed to be. You laugh when you find something funny, even when those around you are still trying to figure it out. Your wonderful patience with everyone. Not just the babies, but with your brothers and me." She sat on his lap, facing him. "Would you take me away? Make love to me? Claim me as your mate?"

"Yes. But I won't make love to you. I will make it *with* you. The two of us, we're a couple. I won't ever rule you. I will offer my opinion, and I know that you'd give it as much consideration as I would yours. I will love you until there is no more breath in my body, and even after death, I will have you in my heart. You are all that I ever wanted in a mate. A person to love. A partner to raise our children with. For all eternity and beyond, you are the only woman I will cherish and love like no other." He grinned at her. "Now, if you don't mind, my love, I want to fuck your brains out."

Allie was laughing all the way up the stairs. He was hungry but thought he could feast on the woman he loved. Beckett, or Beck, as his family was beginning to call him, thought that he had it the best of all. Life.

Chapter 5

Every place his fingers ran over her skin, she felt like he'd marked her. Allie had had sex before, but with Beck making love to her, she thought that was all it had been. Sex. This was making love. Touching. Feeling and tasting each other. The way his skin warmed beneath her own hands. She wanted to explore all of him, taste the parts of him that called to her. Allie wanted to experience this man.

"Your skin is softer than I've ever touched." She moaned when he kissed her breast just above her nipple. "I love the way your nipples tighten and swell. Almost as if they're begging me to taste them."

"Please. Do it." She should have been prepared for his mouth over her breast. Allie knew on some level that he wouldn't just taste. He suckled hard on her nipple, then took her breast entirely into his mouth. "Yes, Beck. Please. I need more."

His pants were undone, the zipper tight against his

cock. When she couldn't get it to pull down, she bypassed the zipper and slid her hand into his pants, wrapping her hand around his thick cock. Beck moaned when she did. A course of amazing feelings sounded out in the room around them.

She realized she was naked but didn't feel chilled. They'd yet to touch the bed, but she felt like she was on the verge of something big. Something monumental that would forever change her. Putting her arms around Beck, he kissed her with passion and hunger. Before she could guess what he would make her feel next, she was lifted up and pressed against the wall.

"I've thought about taking you right here since the first time I thought of you in this room." She looked around. "You've been sleeping in my bed. It's been difficult for me to sleep in another room when I knew that you were just down the hall from me and in my bed."

His cock was at her clit. Each time he moved, she could feel the thickness of him, the veins down the sides of it. The crown was so full she wanted to taste it. Beck lifted her up, taking her breast into his mouth, and slid into her so deep she thought he'd touched her womb.

"Christ, don't move." She couldn't help it. Her body, adjusting to his size, had him crying out. "You're going to end this before I've had a chance to make you come for me. I want to feel you coming all around my —"

She rolled her hips, ending his ability to speak, she thought. When he took her hard, filling her from her hips to her throat, Allie held onto him like her life depended on it. Then he came.

Her body felt turned inside out. Even though she'd not come, her body seemed to need to wait for him. His cock and body did things to her that she'd never experienced before. It wasn't just taking her, but a becoming of one. The two of them melted into a single entity.

When Beck pressed hard against her body, Allie knew she was going to lose it. Her body and mind just snapped out of time and space. The climax that rolled over her was too much. Sliding into a place of sweet smells and darkness, Allie knew forever she'd be safe where she was.

"Are you all right?" She looked at Beck as he leaned over her. They were in the bed, atop the blankets, and the curtains were drawn. Allie stretched and asked him what had happened. "I think you tried to kill us both. That was short but very satisfying. For me. I'm sorry that you didn't get to come more than one time."

She just stared at him. "People come more than one time? Never mind. Don't answer that. If I had come anymore, I think I really would be dead." He kissed her then, and she wrapped her arms around his shoulders. "That was wonderful. I bet you're the best one in your class."

He laughed, and that was what she had intended for him to do. "I was in the top of my class, yes. You're beautiful, all tousled like you are. If you're up to it, I'd love to see you as your cat. I'm betting she's as beautiful as you are."

"Doubtful, but I would like to see what I look like. How do we do this?"

She thought about her cat, the way she seemed to be lurking right there for her. Pressure over her body made her feel like she was falling off the bed, and she looked at Beck. He was laughing.

"Usually, someone will wait for an answer before they shift. Christ, you're more beautiful than I ever imagined. Don't move. If you do, we'll need a new bed and furniture. You're such amazing colors of reds and golds. It makes the black on you— Let me take your picture. You're not going to get it just with me telling you."

He took several pictures of her as she lay on the bed. Twice she had to remind herself that she couldn't stretch out her hand. Her paw, larger than she thought her real hand was, spouted long claws out the tips that she was sure could ruin a bed in less time than she could make it. Beck went to the door that led out onto their deck and opened it for her. Again, reminding her not to let her claws out, Beck also told her that she would have a little trouble walking on four feet rather than just the two.

She's larger than I thought she'd be. Like, look where her head is compared to you. He said she'd weigh more, too, simply because of the muscle mass she had as a tiger. *I guess that makes sense. It's not too hard to walk on four feet. It's like crawling, I think.*

The floor in their bedroom was hardwood and a little slick for her. But she managed to get all the way to the door and the deck beyond without making too much of a fool of herself. The urge to leap over the railing was making her itchy. Looking at the distance to the ground, she decided that she could do it. Running a little, she stretched out her body and soared through the air long enough to hit the grass beneath her.

"Bravo! That was amazing! You did it." She felt like she'd won some sort of contest when Beck called down to her. "I got it on my phone. I couldn't believe it when you just jumped. I think it took Rogen like a month before she got the hang of flying."

It's so amazing feeling this way. Like I could take on a fight and come out on top. Two tigers came out of the woods. Watching them, she figured out who they were by just the way they walked. *It's your dad and Thatcher, isn't it?*

"Yes. Dad saw you leap. He wanted to tell you how much he enjoyed that." They rubbed heads with her. Beck told her they were marking her as their own so that other tigers in the area would know she was a Robinson. "I'm going to shut the door here, and I'll join you."

He leaped over the railing as well. Beck was smooth about it. He also didn't show off. While he was with his dad and brother, Allie explored the new world she'd been given.

What surprised her the most was how much better she could see. It wasn't in color like she'd thought, but in hues. Like red, when it was a living thing. Blues for the trees. It took her a moment to realize that the red thing she was seeing in the wooded area behind the house was a person. Human. Turning back to the men, she backed to them rather than showing her rear to whoever was out there.

There's someone out there. Thatcher told her it was just the wolves that ran the woods. *No. It's a human. I can see the outline of the person. They're nearing the house that's right along the path you came from. I can see the wolves too, but they're not red like the man, I think it is. But they're golden, like you three are.*

Thatcher stood on one side of her, Beck the other. It took what she considered too long to make them believe she was seeing what she was. Finally, aggravated that she had to convince them she was right, she took off at a run toward the person and ran him out of the woods into the yard they were in.

See? Human. The man laid down, curling into the fetal position. The entire time he was there, he was saying he'd not meant to trespass, that he'd only been looking around. It wasn't until she moved closer to him that she was able to see the man was armed. *He has a gun, guys. I'll get it before he figures out a gun is faster than we are.*

Holding it in her teeth, she put it on the deck. Both Thatcher and Beck were staring at her while their dad was laughing. It was an odd sound to hear a tiger laughing, and she went to stand over the man in the event that he got something stupid in his head.

She got the two of you there. Nudging the man on the ground, she asked Thatch if he was able to help her. *I surely can. But I think you can do whatever you set your head to. Leaping over railings like you've been doing it forever. Finding humans that have no business on our land. Not to mention him being here with a gun. I will help you, darling, but I tell you, you've made this old man feel so good.* Thatch went from animal to man in seconds, picking up the gun she'd gotten and pointing it at the person still on the ground. "Now, how about you telling us what you're doing snooping around with a gun in your hands."

Thatcher shifted too and spoke to the man while his dad held the gun on him. Beck came to stand by her, and she wondered if she was going to be in trouble. It was foolhardy of her to run after the man. He could well have shot her, and that would have been the end of her happiness.

How did you see him? I don't mean how, but what made it so you could see him? Even with knowing where to look, neither of us saw him until he started running. She said that he was red, brighter than the things around him. *You saw his body heat then. Not the man himself.*

I guess not, now that you say it like that. He was glowing hot, I think is what you mean. Beck nodded and said that he couldn't do that. *Do you see in color then? I mean, the green of the grass and the tree trunk brown?*

Yes. I'm assuming you don't. You see things by their heat signature or outline. She nodded at him, then said yes. *I don't think any of us can do that. That, my dear mate, is going to make you invaluable for searching things out when none of the rest of us can. I'm wondering what other things you got that the rest of us don't have.*

Is that a bad thing? He explained to her that it was wonderful and that even Rogen had gotten things that none of them had. *So each time someone is changed into a tiger, they get more…what is it called? Power?*

Magic.

They both turned when they heard another voice. It was Rogen, and she didn't look at all happy. She was telling the other two that she had called the police and that she didn't have any more on him than just that he was going to be dead soon. Almost like she'd counted on it, the man started talking about why he was there.

"I was looking for a woman." Rogen told him there were plenty of other women around that he could have spoken to. "Not any woman. Her name is Rogen or something. She had my sister killed a few months ago. April. Bundy was her last name, and she was trying to make sure the world wasn't full of shifters like you guys."

"April Bundy killed her husband, then herself. It was in all the papers how she'd murdered for no reason." Rogen looked at the two of them, then back at the man as she continued. "She had tried to murder a nice family: twin little girls and a little boy. Not to mention their parents. Why on earth would you come here and think to avenge her when she'd nearly killed some very nice people?"

"She wrote me a letter. In it, she told me there were too many monsters here to be taken care of alone and asked me if I'd gather my family up and come help. I was on my way when I heard she'd been murdered." Rogen said suicide. "No. She'd never do that. I'll never believe it. It was you monsters that made her have to kill them. Monsters are taking over the world."

The police arrived just as Allie and Beck went into the house to shift. She supposed they could have done it out there, but the man on the ground was agitated, and she thought his noodle had been played with enough.

Allie had been briefed, they called it, on each of the circumstances that had brought them together. Rogen had nearly died while trying to save a family of five when Mrs. Bundy had taken on her crusade. Anna had been saved when Morgan had killed a man to save her life. Tru had been shot in the hospital taking out a target and had been a patient of Thatcher's before Houston had met her. There wasn't a nice meeting on the Internet or over a pizza among this family's women. She did wonder how they'd describe her meeting Beck when another woman joined the group. Allie had no doubt either there would be at least two more to come around.

Going back into the yard, no one mentioned that she'd seen him or how she'd seen him out there. Nor that she'd chased him into the yard for the others to see. Andrew, the chief, said he recommended putting out more patrols around the houses for a few days.

"I don't know if he acted alone or not, but there isn't any reason to take a chance." Thatcher agreed and said he'd take care of it. "Thank you. The world sure is full of the strangest notions anymore. Don't you think?"

"Yes. I have to agree with you on that one. We had

some idiot out at the hospital area that is being built saying that he was the owner of the land there. Come to find out, he was in not only the wrong county but state too. There is no small number of people anymore that seems to be not carrying a full load of brains." They all laughed.

Allie could tell that Thatcher was upset about something. Whatever it was, she hoped it wasn't about her. When the man was taken away, kicking and screaming about finding that Rogen person, Thatcher and Rogen asked to speak to her.

"No." Thatcher looked shocked. Rogen just smiled. "I don't know what you think I might have done, but I'm in a great mood, and I don't want you shitting on my parade today. They're all lined up to start the band, and you'll just wait to talk to me when it's over."

"You're very weird. Or you've been hanging around my dad a great deal." Thatch told his son to watch himself, or he'd be taking him to the woodshed. "I wasn't insulting you, Dad. Just making an observation. But Allie saved Rogen today. Even after I called her silly for thinking she saw something I'd not. I owe you."

"No, you don't. And I said I didn't want to talk to you." He just laughed, like he'd expected no less from her. "Look. Good, no one got hurt, and that's all we can hope for at the end of the day. I have this odd thing that makes it so I can see heat signatures. Let's not make a huge production out of it. The next time I tell you there is someone out there, just believe me. That's all I need."

"I can handle that." He looked over her shoulder, and she did as well. Beck was shaking his head like he was telling his brother to give it up. "By the way, Allie, welcome to the family."

~*~

Beck was getting his paperwork filed on the last job he'd done. There was good money to be made in doing this sort of work, but it made it less appealing when the people didn't believe him when he had all the facts in a neat row for them, like this last job.

"Tell me about it." He looked up and saw his mom there. Beck loved it when she just dropped everything and came to see him. Today was just as perfect as every other time. "Tell me what has you tensed up. Then I have something I'd like to speak to you about."

"I worked for this company — I can't tell you the name because I don't want you guys boycotting this place too." She said that if it was anything like the salad dressing company, she might not want to know. "No. It's nothing like that. They had me come in and look over their lines. Then while there, he springs the books on me. He told me he didn't think anything was going on with them. He just thought I could find a way for them to cut costs on that as well. I found out about both issues within the first ten minutes of being there. His lovely, much younger wife is not just having fun with the employees, but she's doctoring the books as well."

"Oh my. Does he know that now?" Beck told her he did. "And how did he take the news? Did he tell you how wrong you were?"

"No. I'd had that happen before. The man or woman didn't want to believe their other half was getting some on the side." Mom tisked at him. "I could have said it to you like Rogen or any of the other women. So, instead of just telling him about it, I sort of had him walk in on her and one of the employees."

"Oh, Beck, you didn't." He nodded. "What on earth were you thinking? What if he had had a gun or something. Or tried to kill them both right then and there? That could have gotten you hurt, and Allie would have blamed me."

"What would I blame you for?" Beck smiled at Allie when she joined them in his office. She kissed his mom on the cheek and asked again. "If you're referring to the man that was trying to kill Rogen, I've been thanked enough for that. So, what do you think I need to blame you for?"

"Oh, yes. Thank you for saving my family." Mom told her what he'd done. "I was just asking him how you'd think I raised him if the man had hurt him or something. To do such a thing to the poor man. I think it's bad enough that he has a falling down company, but to find out his wife was with another man…well, that's just not a good way to treat someone."

"Another woman." His mom looked confused but got it. Her face turned a bright red, and Allie laughed. "She thinks it's all right, don't you, love?"

"I would have done it differently, but your way

worked. I'm betting he knew anyway. I would think that if you're an older man and you have a young wife, you gotta think there is something going on with her. But as for blaming you? I'd not do that. What I would do is beat the living shit out of Beck here for getting hurt. Because you know as well as I do that he's been brought up by the best, and if nothing stuck, like making sure he's not hurt at work, then all I can tell you is that you did try."

Mom burst out laughing. It was a hardy laugh, too, like she'd been caught off guard with it. Hugging Allie, she said that she loved her and was so happy she was a part of the family. Mom turned to him and told him that he should respect her opinion more. That Allie was brilliant.

"I agree with you on that. Did she tell you we're babysitting the kids tonight?" She asked which ones. "Houston's brood. Allie and I are going to see if we want children by borrowing some from the others. I thought about just Jimmy, but then I thought we'd just go for it and see if we could handle a pack of them."

Mom smiled and looked at Allie. "If you need some help, I want you to call me. I'd gladly help you out with changing a diaper or two. You'll love it. None of them are walking yet, but the girls can pull themselves up on things. Oh, you will have so much fun with them."

"They're going to be home when this happens. Just watching television, they told us. I think there might be some hanky panky going on, but I didn't ask." Mom told him to behave. "I am. Again, I didn't tell you like the other women would have that they're going to have loud sex. More than likely, all over their home."

"The things you say to your poor mother." Mom stood up and reached for Allie's hand. "Come with me, child. We'll go over there now and see if you can get a head start on the children. Let this one figure it out on his own. I didn't raise him to be mouthy like this either."

"What if they're in foreplay mode right now?" Beck nearly fell off the chair he'd been sitting in when Allie said that to his mother. Every time he looked at his mother, he would laugh all the harder. The look on her face was priceless in the way she just stared, open mouthed, at Allie. Allie just stared back like what she had said was just as normal as rain in the summer.

He would never forget this. Not so long as he lived would he ever let Mom forget it either. With one comment, Allie had rendered his mom speechless. He couldn't wait to tell his brothers about this. They'd not let her live it down either.

"Well, I never." Allie smiled and told her that, obviously, she had at least six times. "Allie Robinson."

He hurt. Beck was sure he might have broken a couple of ribs while he was laughing so hard. Lying on the floor, where he ended up when his mom stormed out of the house, was something else to add to his memories. He'd never seen her so embarrassed in all his life. Allie sat on the chair across from him and laughed too.

"I don't think she's ever going to forgive me for this." He shook his head. "Not that I blame her, but she set herself up for it. Oh my goodness, Beck, I think perhaps I might well have to do something really nice for her to want to hang out with me again. And I think I might have broken you."

Getting up off the floor, he was still laughing. He expected his mom to come back through the door at any moment and tell him that she was never returning. It would be terrible if she did that, but he wasn't sure he could blame her. They had gotten her, but good. Sitting in the other chair, he laughed in little bursts as he spoke to Allie about some other things that had been going on today.

"Remember me telling you about Sam and Jacob, and the kids at school?" She asked if he meant the school that she had worked at. "Yes, that's it. The teachers there have all been fired. The school isn't going to be reopening any time soon, if ever. I was talking to Houston a little while ago, and he told me they were able to get the boys back in the pack school and that they'd let them keep going there until they didn't want to anymore. The principal has been charged with all kinds of things that are going to keep her in prison for a very long time. The nurse will have to serve time, as well. She'll also be doing community work, under supervision, with the county. She'll be working at the county animal shelter. Feeding the animals and cleaning their cages."

"They're having her work with animals? I don't know if I like that any better than her working with kids. At least kids can tell on her." Beck asked her what she would have suggested for her. "You mean besides killing her? I don't know. Perhaps something along the lines of digging graves or even working in a fishery. I did that once. That is not a job I would ever want to repeat."

"I'll talk to Tru. She's the one that asked the judge for her to have some sort of punishment for what she did to her nephews." He watched her work through whatever was in her head. Beck loved to watch her at any project. "Want to tell me what has your forehead all scrunched up?"

"I was talking to Anna about her children. She said it was easy for them to adopt them because of the fact they're Robinsons. We are too." He said he'd been one for a long time. "Don't be a dick. What would you say if I told you I'd like to adopt children? Not just babies—everyone wants them—but older children as well. I know firsthand how it is when you go week after week with people interviewing you and not be taken home. Four isn't very old, but it's painful to see babies get to have parents, and you don't. That's when self-doubting sets in."

"So long as you're happy, I'm happy. I would like to have children with you as well." She told him that she would as well. "Do you know of any children that need someone, or actually us, to love them?"

"I do. They're at the police station now." He asked her why they were there. "The last home they were at, they had some issues and ran away. The older one is fourteen—his name is Conor. The younger, his sister, is twelve, and she goes by Stripes. I'm not sure why that is, but I intend to find out. Would you go with me to see them? Andrew called Tru when I was over working with them, and she told me about it."

"Yes. Right now." Beck was working out in his mind what it would take for them to bring home two teenagers but didn't voice that to Allie. There were rooms set up for anyone that wanted to stay with them, but he was positive they would need clothing and other things. More excited than he'd been when they'd embarrassed his mom, he smiled at Allie. "This might be just the thing to get you out of the doghouse with Mom. And Dad will be over the moon to have a grandchild old enough to fish."

"How much do you want to bet they've never had anyone take them fishing, Dad? I've never been either." He was still standing there when she turned around at the car. "What?"

"I'm going to be a dad. You and I are going to be parents." She told him not if he didn't get his ass in gear. "Yes. All right. But if we don't like them or they're snarky, we'll walk away."

"Sure. I want to see you do that." He had a feeling she was making fun of him, but he chose to ignore it. "I don't know, but I'm sure this truck isn't going to be big enough for two more people in it. Teenagers don't like to touch each other."

Allie filled him in on the kids as they made their way to the station house. They had been in seven foster homes since they'd been orphaned three years ago. They'd been raised by their grandma, who had died in her sleep one night. The parents of the kids were out of the picture.

"Rogen looked it up for me just in case we decided to go see them. What out of the picture means is that they're both serving double life sentences for murder. No chance for parole, nor do they have visitation rights. The kids haven't seen them since they were left at home the night they killed a family of four for their car." He asked her if they'd had a hard life. "It didn't seem like it, but there is no way of telling until we talk to them. They've been pushed around a great deal in the system. Mainly because they don't want to be separated, which is making it difficult for them. No one wants to take on two teenagers at the same time, I'm thinking."

"Who else besides Rogen knows about us going to see them?" Allie said that Tru and Anna knew, but they said they'd not say anything. "Rogen even suggested that we keep the kids with just us for a few days to see if we can make it fit. I don't know what she thought we'd do with them if they didn't. But I have confidence in our ability to take care of them. Don't you?"

"Yes." He thought about what he'd told his mom about sitting the kids. "You know that we're not really watching the kids, don't you? I mean, I was just getting at Mom before you nearly had her head exploding."

"Yeah, I knew. Boy, she was fun to play with." They both laughed right up until they pulled in front of the station house. "This is it. Our last night of freedom. Are we sure about this?"

"Yes. I am as sure about this as I am with my love for you." Neither of them got out of the car. "Are you afraid? Because I'm terrified."

"Right there with you. But we won't know shit until we go and meet them."

Allie got out of the truck first. He thought she was braver than he was because not only was he having second thoughts, he was having fourth and fifth thoughts as well. Getting out, he took her hand as they entered the building. They'd be parents in about an hour if he didn't miss his bet. And he couldn't wait.

Chapter 6

Conor held his sister while they sat in the cell. This was the third time they'd been brought here after running away, and he decided the next time they weren't going to run in any direction that led back to here. He wasn't sure how that would work, but he was going to try his best. They kept returning them, and that wasn't helping them be safe at all.

"Conor, there are some people here to see you two. Are you going to behave yourself this time?" He shook his head. Behaving himself nearly got his sister killed. "Yeah, I didn't think you would. Something you should understand about this couple, they're not going to take your shit. You mess with them, and you might find yourself wishing you'd not. I've already explained to them that you get mouthy and mean. I'm telling you right now, Conor, you'd be well set up if you were to allow these people in—"

"They hurt us." Andrew got down on his knees in

front of Stripes. Holly was her real name, but the last home kept calling her that for some insane reason. Andrew asked Holly to look at him. Her black eye and cut lip made his blood boil each time he saw it. They'd locked Conor away from her to get at her, and that hurt him badly. "They wanted me to do things with the man."

"I know, sweetie. I've had them picked up and put into a cell, too, in another stationhouse. The next county over is going to deal with them pretty quick. I'm so sorry you had to go through that." She turned her head into his shirt. Conor felt the need to lash out at the policeman for taking them back there over and over. "I will tell you that Allie and Beckett are the nicest people you can meet. They come from a long line of nice people too. Beckett's mom is one you don't mess with, and her boys, all six of them, are afraid of her."

"Why can't we just stay at the home where they took us when our grandma died? I didn't want to be taken out of there, Mr. Andrew." Conor wanted to know the same thing. They didn't want to be adopted if all there was out there were perverts and dick heads. "We wasn't bothering no one."

"No, you weren't, honey, but you can't stay there forever. You need a home that is good for you. All right?" She didn't answer him, and Conor looked at the older man. "Conor, you have to give these people a chance."

"I hope he will, but I have a feeling he's not going to. Are you, Conor?" The woman came into the cell where they were sitting, and Andrew left them. "My name is

Allie Robinson, and this is my husband, Beck. I know your names are Conor and Stripes. I don't understand why you'd be called that but nothing much more."

"Her name is Holly. Don't act all friendly to us. We know you won't want to keep us both. Well, I'm not going to let you take her from me so that you can let that man mess with her. You hear me, bitch?" Allie looked up at her husband, then back at him. "I'm not afraid of either of you. We will run away from you too if you pull any shit like the last place did."

The slap to his cheek startled him. When she hit him the second time, he stood up. After being told to sit, he did so before he realized he was making a stand. Conor wanted to hit her back, but he was afraid of Beck. Men could be really mean when you hurt their women.

"You speak to me like that again, and I'll ground you for the rest of the summer. I've done nothing to you to warrant such behavior, and I won't tolerate you taking your shitty mood out on me. Understand me? Also, you're going to cool your jets. I've only introduced ourselves to you, and you've flown off the handle like I've told you that you're going to be slave labor for us. You're not, in case that is going through your mind. Now, are you willing to keep that trap of yours closed and listen to us?" Conor nodded. He realized then that he had it wrong. He should be more afraid of the woman. "Now. We're going to start over. My name is Allie Robinson, and that is my husband, Beck. Holly, since your brother is being a little shit, why don't you tell me a little about yourself."

Conor had no idea what to do now. Usually, when he was mouthy with one of the adults, they'd say they didn't want them. Not only had this woman hit him, but she hadn't raised her voice nor her fist. The slaps weren't that bad, and he did really deserve it. Conor, never one to show tears, felt them well up in his eyes as he turned to the man, Beck.

"The people there tried to rape Holly. They locked me up so I couldn't get there to save her. But I got out by busting the door down." Beck asked him if either of them had been hurt. "Not too much. Holly was tied up, and it cut into her some. I've been trying to keep the wound clean, but there isn't much in the way of water and soap just lying about."

"I have two brothers that are doctors. I'll have one of them look at the two of you when we get back to the house. Do you guys have anything other than what you came here with?" The man was talking to him like he was a person, not like he was nothing but a bug under his shoe. Conor felt his eyes fill with tears again when the man asked him how badly he'd been hurt too.

"I've been trying my best to make sure Holly wasn't hurt. But all people want to do is have sex on her. I'm just a kid, but they should know better, don't you think?" Beck stood up and pulled him up from the seat. Thinking that he was going to be hurt by the large man, Conor stiffened his body for the blows. But all he did was hug him. Tightly too.

Conor only cried at night, when the lights were off,

and his sister was asleep. He didn't have the strength to hold them back anymore and let them flow like they were hot lava making his eyes boil over. Beck held him as tightly as he'd allow him to while Allie did the same to Holly.

He didn't know how long Beck held him. And really, Conor decided he didn't care either. It had been so long since anyone had bothered with him in a nice way that he would have stayed there being held all day if he could have. However, when he pulled back, Beck didn't brush him off like he thought he would but kept his hand on his shoulder lightly, like they were the best of friends. Beck asked Holly if she was all right with having Andrew take some pictures of her wounds.

"They had a lady police officer do that already." Allie said that was wonderful. Then she asked if they were hungry. "Yes, ma'am. It's been a couple of days before we left since we got any food. They were making us weak, they told us."

Anger. It came off the woman like the lava hot tears that he'd cried. Conor reached for his sister to pull her away from Allie, but she smiled at him. It was a real one too. Not a bit of evilness was in her eyes. Conor had never been so confused around two people in his life. They weren't acting at all like anyone ever had with them before.

"I'm not angry with you two. But I might have to teach a couple of people what it is to be responsible for another person's life. I want you two to know this right now. There will never be a time when we hold food from you. We'll never turn away a hug. And you can bet your sweet asses that you guys are going to be taken care of." Conor laughed. He was nervous, but her cursing was just like he thought someone would talk. Not holding back. Conor told Beck that when he asked. "Wait until you meet the rest of the family. You two will hear cursing like you've never heard before. But you'll have a set of grandparents and aunts and uncles that will be there for you too."

"You're acting like you're going to take us home with you. Don't you want to, I don't know, have a dry run or something? The other people did." Allie looked at Beck and asked him if he needed a dry run. He smiled at his wife and told her he was good. "You two are weird. Do you know that?"

"We are. And yes, we know it. I was a child of the system too. It didn't get any better after I was adopted either. No one tried to rape me, but they did hurt me mentally, as well as verbally. I already want the best for you guys. Oh, I forgot to mention, you'll already have lots of cousins. Come on, Beck, let's feed these guys and take them home. Tomorrow we'll have to get them other things to wear, but for now, I just want to get to know them."

The pizza place wasn't very busy, but the owner came out from the back when they entered to give Beck and Allie a hug. She asked after someone that Conor didn't hear her name, and they were seated in an area that just held them. Beck handed them menus and told them to get whatever they wanted. Conor didn't even know what he wanted, not having had pizza from a restaurant before.

"I've invited my family to come and eat with us. Mom and Dad, my parents, will be here first. They don't know that we're going to adopt you, so I would appreciate it if you would put your best foot forward for them. I'm asking you nicely, Conor, not to piss my mom off. She'll be both your best friends if you allow her to be." He lowered his head and felt his shame. He'd not asked him to be nice to him or with Allie. Just his mom. For some reason, that hurt him all the way to the tips of his toes. "Are you listening to me?"

"Yes, sir. I'm sorry I acted the way I did. I have no excuse for acting like that against you two." Beck said his name, and when he looked at him, he told him that he had every right to be hurt with people. No one had treated them kindly. "No, sir. No one has cared a bit for either one of us. Not even our parents."

"I'm sorry about that. Both of us are. The moment we heard about you, we both considered you ours. Allie told you that she'd been a part of the system, and that's the truth. She wasn't abused, not like you guys were, but she didn't get the love she already has for the two of you." Conor looked at Allie as she read over the menu with Holly. His sister was smiling, something that he'd missed until now. "I'm not going to blackmail you into anything either. Nor will I try to mislead you into something that will harm either of you. I want you to know that we're nice people and only want what is best for the two of you."

"I kind of figured that out. That you're nice people, I mean."

There was a loud voice at the front of the restaurant, and Conor reached for his sister. He'd been doing that for so long, protecting her, that he did it now whenever she was afraid. But seeing the look on her face when she stared at the man coming toward them, he relaxed for a moment to see how this would go. The man looked like a giant coming at them. But he looked so much like Beck that Conor knew this was his dad.

"I surely do have me a pickle of a time finding a place to park here sometimes. I knew when I was able to get me one close up that we'd be about the only ones in here. What did you have to pick up at the station house? Boy, oh boy, Tru surely did give them a piece of her mind." The older man looked at him and smiled. "I guess you found you another date than me and your mom. She's on that phone of hers making arrangements for our vacation coming up. Who might you be, young man?"

"Your grandson." Conor put out his hand and watched the man as he continued. "I'm Conor, and this is my sister Holly. We're going to be kids of Beck and Allie. I guess he told you, right?"

"No. No, he didn't." The man looked at Beck, then back at him. "He never said a word about me having grandkids today. I have me a bunch of them now. But you two, you and your sister, are the oldest. Can I have me a hug, young Conor?"

It hurt his ribs a little to be held by this man. He hugged like he meant business. When he let him go, Beck asked him if he was all right, and he had to confess that he wasn't rightly sure. Lifting up his shirt, he could see that the bruising there was getting bigger. It made him slightly sick to his belly to see how bad it really looked. Then he couldn't breathe in enough air to make his lungs work.

"Jumping Jehoshaphat. Who did that to you, son?" He tried to tell him who had done it and why, but he was having some trouble breathing. When he found himself on the floor with his shirt up around his neck, he looked at Allie, who was right there over him. Grandda was telling him he was sorry. "I didn't mean to break him. Lordy, you'll never let me watch him now."

"Look at me, Conor. That's it. Just think about breathing. Very slowly, right now. All right?" He nodded, then stopped. "No. Breathe, honey. Breath in and out. Not too much air, but you do it until it hurts, all right. In and out. Dawson is here now. He's a doctor, and he's going to look at you. Don't close your eyes. Breathe."

Her voice calmed him down. It was like she had a direct line to his lungs, too, so that they worked better. It hurt like the dickens, but it was feeling better all the time. When a man came into his line of sight, he smiled at him too.

"I'm Dawson. Your new uncle. I'm going to press on your ribs just a little, all right? You just keep breathing like your mom told you to do." Conor looked at Allie. He wanted her to be his mom. Even after embarrassing her by making a scene in a restaurant, she didn't yell at him. "She won't yell at you for having some broken ribs, Conor. No one should do that. How are you feeling?"

"I hurt, but I don't want to cry. I don't want to embarrass them anymore." Dawson said he hadn't done that. Like he said, it wasn't his fault he'd been hurt. "That other man, he hit me all the time. Will you help me with the pain? I'm thinking I might be sick from it."

"I'm going to give you just a little bit, Conor. Enough to take the edge off the pain. Next time you're hurt, you'll have to tell us. Though I doubt very much, you'll be hurt this badly ever again. Unless you play football. Do you play?" He said he didn't know how. "Well, you stick with this family, and we'll help you out with that. Now, you're going to feel just a little pinch."

The pain didn't go away, not all of it, but he could breathe around it now. When he was set up, he noticed that everyone was standing up watching him. Allie asked him if he was feeling all right for dinner or did he want to go on home.

"I'd rather stay if I can. I'm sorry." She ruffed up his hair and told him he was fine. When he was helped to stand, he was put in a booth seat next to his granddad. He told him he was sorry for hurting him. "You didn't. You gave me the best hug I've ever had, Grandpa. I can call you that, can't I?"

"You surely can. Yes, sir, you surely can."

The pizza was brought out. Conor couldn't eat all that much—he was suddenly exhausted. Finding a soft spot up against his grandda, Conor decided to take a little nap. He knew he'd feel better after a little nap.

~*~

Beck carried Conor up to the bedroom he was going to be using. They'd have to redecorate it. Well, do something with it besides having just furniture in the room. He'd not even gotten around to having any blinds or curtains put in. His mom was hot on his heels as he laid the young boy in the big bed.

"My goodness, he sure is tiny in this bed, don't you think?" Beck told his mom that he thought both of them were underweight. "I believe you're right—that poor little Holly. Every time something louder than a bump happened, she was looking for a place to hide. Both of them have been having a hard time of it, haven't they, son?"

"Yes. Tru and Allie, with the other two, are looking into a couple of things. Andrew told us what the kids had told him when they were picked up. They had tied Holly to the bed and had men lined up to take their turn with her. Conor was locked up in the shed out back. It's not hard to imagine what would have happened to them had he not broken out of the shed and gotten in there and saved her from her fate." Mom cried a little, her hand over her mouth to keep the words she wanted to say well hidden. "I want to tell you that Allie smacked him twice before you got to the restaurant. He deserved it, hands down, but if he gets mouthy with you, I want to know about it."

"You will. But I'll take care that he doesn't." He knew that she would too. His mom was going to love these guys if she didn't already. "Beckett, I want to hunt those people down and make sure they understand that they messed with the wrong family."

"I think if you wanted to help the women, they'd let you. They're in the basement of Thatcher's house plotting now." She left him after kissing Conor on the forehead.

They didn't have anything for the kids to wear to bed. Holly had been given a long shirt of Allie's to put on. Conor would have to sleep in his underwear. But Beck wasn't all that comfortable taking his jeans off him. He was afraid the kid would wake up and think the worst was happening to him. Reaching out to Dawson, he asked him how deeply Conor was under.

Deep. Why? He told him. *Oh. I can understand that. But it's doubtful he'll wake up. Not only has the kid been hurt, but it's also doubtful he's gotten a good night's sleep in a while. The meds I gave him when we left the restaurant will keep him out for a while. I'd say you're safe with disrobing him. If you've already got them into bed, big brother, I'll just come over tomorrow to check on them. There isn't any point in waking them up.*

He didn't hurry through taking them off, fearful of him waking. But the more he pulled the pants down, the more wounds he could see on the boy. He'd taken quite a beating. Telling Dawson about them, he repeated that he'd be right over in the morning to have a look.

He also told Allie, who relayed the information to the others. *His legs are so bruised it looks like he's been dipped in blue and black paint. His arms are also badly bruised. I don't know how he was able to move, much less take care of his sister the way he did.*

I'm going to kill them. He didn't even bother telling Allie she couldn't do that. He wanted the same thing. *They had taken an ad out for men to pop a cherry, it says. The biggest bidder won. Christ, to think that the system paired any child or children with this couple is beyond me.*

I take it, then, that you've found them. She told him they were currently in jail but would be released soon. *Why?*

Rogen is going to make it happen. He didn't ask. Beck was sure that he didn't want to know any of the details. Also, he had a feeling that no one would ever just happen to come across their bodies, nor would anyone know what happened to them. Or care, for that matter. *Are the kids in bed?*

Yes. I've taken off Conor's pants after checking with Dawson to make sure he was sleeping well enough. Mom put Holly to bed. She even told her some things about what she had planned for the three of them. They're settled in all right here. You just be careful. She assured him that she wasn't going to go out on this one. None of them were. *I think that's an excellent plan. No one can come back later and say you did it.*

Beck went to the living room when he closed the connection to Allie. He could still feel her, but she told him that they were working on something, and he didn't want things to go badly for any of them.

After seeing nothing on the television that he wanted to involve himself in, he went to his office. There was always plenty there to occupy his mind. After setting up the spreadsheet that he used when he was grading a place he'd worked in, he pulled out his notes and got to work.

Sixteen months ago, he'd worked in an office building that had needed some work on production time. They were a company that would help other companies sell shares of their stock for a large profit. He wasn't entirely sure why that was necessary, but they seemed to have been making it work for them. After spending three days working in the office, he discovered what most of their issues were. It was one of those things that making it better for their employees had backfired.

The owner, a man by the name of Horacio Carpenter, was a good employer. When he made a large profit off sales, he would share it with the people who worked for him. Several times a year, he would also upgrade their office space to reflect whatever the employees thought would make their jobs easier. He'd spoiled them entirely too much. There were so many perks that the people working there would use them instead of working. Hot food when they wanted. Exercise equipment to take off the pounds after their hot meals. He'd even put in places for them to take a nap—power naps, he had called them. Everything someone would want was put there for them to use. And they did, to the point of not getting one hour of work put in.

"I never thought it would come to that. I mean, they were so excited about having things to do to keep their minds fresh." Beck had told him that they were more than likely, not realizing they were missing so much work. "I would like to believe that, but right now, all I can think about is how they've taken my kindness and turned it against me. I'll have it all removed."

"Not all at once." Horacio asked him why not. It was making him lose money. "Yes, it is. But if you take it all out at once after just putting it in, you'll have everyone quit, thinking you're a selfish man. Take out the larger things first—the exercise equipment, for starters. You can tell them that the insurance for having them there is a little more than you anticipated. Something that shows you've had to cut back because of the cost, that sales aren't what they used to be."

"They're not." Beck told him they had no way of knowing that if he didn't tell them. "So, in addition to cutting back on some of the things, I should tell them that we're not as in the black as we used to be? Without a reason."

"That's it precisely. You've made them your partners so far. There also isn't any reason they shouldn't know that they're not doing nearly as well because sales are down. Also, you could mention the bonus share that you get. Something along the lines that it might not be there because of production. Don't point fingers, just lay it out there like you would to anyone else." Horacio said he liked that idea. "Good. You let me know when you need help taking out the equipment, and I'll have someone come over and help you out."

That had been last year. Today he got his bonus check for the profit the owner got when production was taken care of. It was more than he thought he'd get. Beck was happy for Horacio and his stocks company.

Allie came in about midnight. Not only had he gotten a good start on his work for tomorrow, but he'd been able to send out six reports that had been gathering dust on his desk, as well as figured out which project he was going to work on next. He smiled at her when she entered his office.

"It's all taken care of." He asked her if she was all right. "I am. Some very nasty people were removed from this world, and my kids are going to be safe from them. Have you found out anything else that I might like to know? Not just the kids, but something better than what I saw in the last few hours. Good news, please."

"I love you." She grinned at him and sat on his lap after pulling his chair back from his desk. "Good news… let me think. Oh, I spoke with Shane earlier, and he said to tell you congrats on the kids, and he has plenty of room for our kids to go to his school as well. They're going to have to be tested for which class they'll be in, but that won't be an issue."

"I'm glad the school there is able to take care of them. I don't think I want to ever stick our kids in a private school. I know there are some pretty amazing ones out there, but I'm a little soured on them right now." He leaned over and picked up the envelope that had been delivered today. "What's this?"

"You killed a monster when you killed Holland. The vampire committee, I'm not sure what they call themselves, has turned all his worldly goods into a cashier's check for you. They want you to have it, as he is no longer at a place where he'd be able to use it." He laughed. "That was how they put it. No longer at a place where he can use it."

"I just wanted to get away from him. I didn't mean for them to reward me for this." Beck told her that was what he told them as well, that she'd not want it for the same reason. "He didn't strike me as having all that much. There wasn't even any power in the place where he took me. How about we use it to make the kids' rooms nice for them?"

"I'm game for that. However, if it's not enough, we have the funds to take care of it." She nodded and opened the envelope. The look on her face told him that it was considerably more than enough to redo the rooms. She didn't say anything when she handed it over to him. "Good Christ, honey, we could buy them their own school."

The cashier's check was for just a smidge over six million dollars. With the check that he'd gotten from his bonus just today, they had in checks just over thirteen million dollars. Grinning, he handed her his check and asked her what she wanted to do with their found money.

"How about we have it invested for our children and our future children? That way, they can go to college and not have to worry about working." He told her that was an excellent idea. "I think so as well. But this is still going to be a lot of money. No matter how you look at it, we'd have to have sixty kids, raise them, and put them through college, and still more than likely not use even half of this. What about a fund? Or a home dedicated to children without parents? An adoption agency that does things by the book, and does the necessary background checks too?"

They agreed that they'd do that. He wasn't sure what sort of red tape they'd have to muddle through, but with Rogen at the computer, they thought they could get it taken care of without much in the way of issues. It was nearing two in the morning when they went up to bed.

Beck was sure the moment his head hit the pillow, he was going to be out. It had been both an exciting and stressful day, and he was just too tired to get up in arms about it. Ending his day by looking in on the children made him smile. Falling into bed, he didn't even have time to pull the covers up and over himself.

Chapter 7

"Allie? Wake up." She sat up, her neck pinching her a little when she did. Looking at Tru, she told her she was sorry. "No need to be. You and I both know why none of us got any sleep. By the way, you have what looks like an M-16 on your forehead and a Glock on your cheek. Did you make these?"

"Yes. Once I got to read over the manual, I figured out that if I could shrink down the size of the guns to match the scale I'm going to use, they won't seem so out of place when I put them to the board. The specs on the weapons were easy enough to find. I just had to get them the size I wanted them to be." She handed the rifle to Tru. "The printer is awesome for doing this. I started out by using it to make things I could attach to the other things we got, but then I realized that nothing was to scale. I think having it look like you want it is going to be important. The blocks are easy enough to shave off, thanks to Thatch fixing them for me."

Each of the blocks were now marked with their sizes. The scale she was using was one-twelfth the size of actual crime scenes. Arriving at that had been harder than she thought it should have been.

"So these blocks, you have them fixed up with windows as well as doors. Is that necessary?" Allie laughed and took the one that Tru had picked up. "They're nice. But I think a little over the top."

"Thatch did that. He and Conor were working together on them, and Holly wanted to help. She was the one that did the windows on things for me. She told me that having them look just like blocks would be boring." Tru smiled back at her. "They're fitting in well, I think. I miss seeing them sometimes."

The kids had been with them for just over a week. Every night she'd get up several times just to check on them, to make sure they were actually still hers and Beck's. Then last night, Rogen had called them in for a hit. It was all she'd been able to do today to keep her eyes open.

"What are you working on next?" Allie told her she was just making things so she'd have them at this point. "This is amazing work, Allie. I know I keep telling you that, but it's wonderful to have you take a crime scene or whatever we need and make it work for us. I've never been so happy to get specs on something so that I can see what you make of it."

"Getting it organized has been the most difficult part. But once I got the shelving I needed and the bins, it was easy to get things in the right places to use. Thatch has been great coming by and working on the little things with me." Tru told her how he loved working with her. "He's funny. Most of the time, he just works away without talking much. Then he'll get on a story and talk for hours. I don't know which one I like better, the quiet or the noise."

"I can't believe you get him to be quiet. The man can talk your arm off. He seems to be having fun with all the grandbabies too. I put your kids in there with them. Conor and Holly were lucky in having you there when they needed it."

"I'm the one that considers myself lucky. We still have to work with Holly. She doesn't like being alone. I don't blame her, but Dawson suggested we let her see a therapist. Perhaps talking to someone will help. Conor gets mouthy at times—not as much as he did those first couple of days. I think that instead of fighting, he lashes out with words. It's all either of them understand when they're afraid. To stand up and hurt the other person." Tru asked her if she needed anything with them. "Not yet. Conor has expressed a desire to come here and look around, but he's grounded at the moment. He lied to us about his homework. I hated doing that more than I did anything that I've done with them so far."

"They need that. Just the right amount of balance between getting away with something and going too far. Me? I go too far all the time." They both laughed, and it felt good. "Don't second guess yourself with telling them the rules, Allie. Mine are just babies, and I'm laying down rules now too. And seeing you two with older kids is helping the rest of us with raising our kids."

"You mean how to not make the same mistakes?" Tru told her they were all going to make mistakes. It was what they did about it that showed the kind of people they raised. "I hope we're doing a good job of this. I'd hate to think we're raising little monsters that will kill us in our sleep some night."

"They'd never do that." Allie didn't think they would either. But she was worried about them. It seemed like the more she tried to be a good parent to them, the worse she was at it. It made her want to cry all the time. "Beck has picked up on it fast. I saw him with them the other day at the ice cream shop. He doesn't allow them to eat sweets all the time, does he?"

"No. It was a celebration of sorts. Conor learned how to use the riding mower, and he paid him. That was what he wanted to do with his money. Celebrate with his family." She asked her where she had been. "I was with them. Maybe you just missed me going to the bathroom. But it was a lot of fun. And his pride in doing a job well done was worth the spoiled dinner."

Allie got back to work on her projects. The printer pen was working out better than she'd ever thought it would. She now had an array of weapons and other things that could be used as one—knives from a kitchen block. Allie had even figured out blood pools. That had taken a little more time than she'd meant for it to. Finally, she'd made it just a circle with other pieces that could be added to it for running blood.

Looking at the specs she'd been given yesterday, she thought she was ready to tackle it. There were different elements in this one that she'd not worked with before. The weapons had only been a part of it. She now had a flower garden, as well as things like a bicycle that she needed. Laying out the groundwork, she thought of nothing else but putting the scene together just like she'd been told it had been by not just pictures but the officers who had been there. The little van she was using for the car was just put in place when Beck joined her. He asked her what she was doing.

"The neighbor, Mr. Grant, told the police that the man who lives across from him, from the Honeywell family, ran over his child on purpose. That Mr. Honeywell had seen his child there on his bike, as he'd spoken to the child before getting into the car and running over not only the child several times, but the bike too. I'm putting it together to see if the man that made the accusation can really see the face of the man in the van. I'm thinking he can't, but then I'm not moving anything around to look just yet." He asked her if the child had died. "Yes. Internal injuries. The coroner said it wasn't consistent with the child being run over with a car, much less several times, as Mr. Grant stated. So that's why I'm doing this. Grant said that Honeywell backed over him three times too. The coroner said he can tell from what he is working with that the child had been hit with a force like a car, but not run over. Now, since we know he lied about seeing that, we're wondering if he could have seen the gleeful look on Mr. Honeywell's face when he did it."

"I didn't think Rogen and you guys did this sort of work." She told him what she was doing. "That's good. Working with some of the local agencies is really good. You never know when you might need them."

"That's pretty much what Tru and Rogan said. I guess we'll see." She looked over her notes again, lining things up that she had written down from the police report. Mr. Grant she had put in his house, where he claimed he'd been, as a small stick figure that she had decided worked as well as anything else. There wasn't a person in the van, only a head that had been made by her. "Okay, what do you see?"

"I see that there isn't any way that Grant could see the face of the man in the car." She said that was only part of what she was looking for. "I'm not even sure if you're asking me how he was able to see into the other yard at all. If you look from his position, you can clearly see that the fencing is in his way."

It wasn't fencing, but a brick barrier. Honeywell had put it in his yard the first year they lived in this place to keep his flowers safe from the kids along the sidewalk. Taking a step back from the entire thing, she could also see that the man across the street wouldn't have been able to even see the side of the van, where he said the kid had been. His entire claim was wrong.

"A child is still dead, but this man's claim of the father

doing it and him seeing him is bogus." Allie looked over her notes and then at the scene again. Picking up the phone, she went out on a limb and called the coroner for the state. "I'm working on this case for Mr. Honeywell's attorney, Mr. Glass, and I'm wondering if the young victim could have been hit someplace else and then made his way to the family home?"

"I was just about to call you, Agent. I've had some of the officers here go out and do some measuring for me. There isn't any way the Honeywell vehicle would have done the damage to the young boy. First of all, he would have had to have been going about sixty when he was hit to have done the kind of damage that was done. You were correct, I'm thinking too, in that young Honeywell was thrown, not run over. Also, the Honeywell bumper doesn't line up with the boy's leg injuries. We're looking into what sort of cars might well be the one it could be." She told him what she thought. "Grant? Well, he is pushing this through pretty hard. And from what I can tell, there…. Let me send an officer from here to his home and have a look at his car. I think that might be the best way to settle this in both our minds."

After she hung up, she felt better about this entire scene. She'd leave this one set up, in the event there were any questions about it, and moved to the next table. Allie loved having this much work to do. It kept her busy and also kept her mind off things that she didn't want to think about right now.

"Do you want to talk about it?" She glanced at Beck,

then went back to work. "You've been stressing out about something since last night. Why don't you tell me so you can work through it? I promise you, I will only listen unless you ask me a question."

"It really doesn't have a great deal to do with me. A little, mind you, but not nearly like it does for Tru. Her kids being hurt when I was at the school." Beck told her he knew about it. "Yes, well, she found out yesterday that the school board is going to rehire the people she had arrested. Some of them are still pending a trial, but according to the information she got yesterday, their jobs are being held for them for when they return. Even with the threat of her not supporting the school anymore, they said that it's fine; they'll just get other supporters. Then, when she threatened them with a lawsuit that would hit the papers, he pointed out to her that she couldn't do that according to her contract with the school."

"What is it that you want us to do?" She turned to him, wondering how she'd gotten so lucky to have someone like him in her life. "You have it all worked out in your head. I know you well enough to have figured out that part of you. Not only do you have it planned out, but I have a feeling you might well know what the outcome will be."

"I don't know for sure the outcome, but I have a good idea what I'd like for it to come out as." She sat on the bench she'd been using to stretch out on. "You will help me, right? I mean, a great deal of my outcome will depend on your help."

"I will do whatever you need for me to do. So long as I get to brag about it to my brothers." She smiled at him. "Thank you. That alone, and bragging rights, makes me want to do anything you want."

Allie told him of her plan. The entire way she had it laid out. Beck asked her questions about some of the things she had in her mind and corrected a couple more. Since she had little dealings with the sort of people she was about to go up against, she was glad for his input. As soon as the two of them had it all lined up, they went to see Tru.

She would only know the outline of what she was going to say and do to these people. Tru was jealous again of her way of thinking. She also begged her to take a gun. Finally, relenting only in that she'd take it if it was the only way Tru would allow her to go, she put it in her back pocket. Tru had a way of getting guns into places that wouldn't normally allow them to be present. She loved working with these women.

~*~

"All she told me was that we're to stay right here with you and watch the monitors. There was mention of her getting the members to turn over some of their stock in the school, but she was really vague on how or why she was doing that. I guess we're going to find out." Tru didn't know a lot of details, but having Allie go to the school instead of her might save a few lives.

It had made her feel as if Allie wasn't going there with the intent to kill. However, having her armed would make sure that she'd at least have some way of defending herself if the shit were to hit the fan. And it was Tru's thoughts that usually the shit did hit the walls, people, and anything else around when it came to stupid people.

Enrolling her children in the pack school was working out better than she could have hoped it would. It wasn't that she hadn't trusted the pack school, but she had been afraid that someone would come for her kids to make her do something she didn't want to, and that would kill a lot of people. The private school had things in place that would keep not just her boys safe, but the teachers and anyone else there as well. It never occurred to her that her kids would be harmed more inside the school walls than out.

"Do you know why they're having this meeting?" Tru looked over at Rogen. "You looked like you were about to get physical for a minute, and I thought I'd pull you out of it. But do you know why they're meeting today?"

"No. The only reason she was able to figure it out was that Thatcher hacked into their system for us yesterday when she came to me. By the way, Thatcher is getting really good at this kind of stuff too. I think he just needs to relax more and have a little more confidence in himself when he finds something." Rogen said she told him that all the time and he just told her that he loved her. "Sounds like Houston."

Anna wasn't working with them today. She had some work she was doing with Morgan. The two of them were forever working together on things that would improve the way families were able to get funding when they needed it. With the colder weather coming up, Anna was seeing that people signed up for energy help as well as anything else that might be out there for them. Next year, they were hoping to have a lot of these people working at full-time jobs.

"Look, there she is. I thought Beck was going to go with her." Tru told her that was what she'd said, then asked her to turn it up. She didn't want to miss a word of it. "I'm recording it too. I know she told me not to, but if it's needed—like she has to kill them all—then I want to be able to say they started it."

"How old are you? Five? They started it?" The two of them laughed, and she watched her new sister-in-law. "She's looking very confident. Oh, before I forget, we're not allowed to speak to her. She thinks it will make her second guess what's she's doing. So we're just to watch and keep our traps shut. Not her words, but that's what she meant by it."

"I'm sure she did. She's so outspoken like that." They watched her as she entered the room. The volume was turned up loud enough for them to hear. Tru decided that Allie's soft-spoken voice should scare a man to death if he knew what lurked under her pretty hair. "She's not going to get what she wants. She's not showing enough force. But it is fun to watch her try."

Tru didn't know, but she thought Rogen was wrong, not that she'd tell the other woman. Even with as good friends as they were, Rogen could still take her down.

Laughing a little to herself, she watched Allie play with the men in the room with her.

~*~

"What the blue blazes are you doing in here? This is a private meeting, and you're not invited. Who the hell let you in anyway?" Allie told the man, who she thought was Clarkson, that she'd invited herself. "Well, you can just uninvite yourself. This is a meeting you're not invited to."

"I know you." Allie nodded at the man next to her. "You used to work for us — the cook or something. If you want to keep your job, you'd better get your butt out of here right now. This meeting is to discuss who is staying and who isn't."

"Good. I'd hate to have crashed a meeting on how you're going to be spending the money that you've stolen. I guess stolen isn't the right word for it. Misappropriated, perhaps? Or embezzled? Both those words apply, don't they, Mr. Clarkson?" He told her he didn't know what she was talking about. "Sure, you do. You have several accounts all over the country that you can get to at a moment's notice. Then there is the account in the Cayman Islands."

Allie reached out to Beck, the only one of the Robinsons she wanted to speak to while there, and told him to contact Rogen now. She only hoped this would work. Beck told her that if she got him to think about something, they could search his mind for the information and use it against him.

He has three accounts in the Caymans. I'm having Rogen look for them now. Good job. Also, there is money in ten different accounts around the country, just like we thought there would be. Allie was feeling better now that things were finally coming together. *Also, you should know that they're recording this so that if anything happens, they have proof. I'm sure they can edit out what they don't want seen.*

Okay. I'm working, so be ready. She was sure it was going to come to the point where she needed his help. Actually, she was looking forward to having him come in with guns blazing, so to speak.

"Mr. Clarkson, you've been taking money from the school since its inception. That is the main reason you've been hiring below standard teachers." Clarkson told her she didn't know what she was talking about. "Don't I? Three of the teachers on staff have criminal records of child abuse. One of them has a conviction for bank robbery. The first-grade teacher, Miss Mann, should have retired years ago. Having a teacher in her seventies is wonderful, but only if she is able to make it to the bathroom on time. She's incontinent most of the time, and there have been complaints of her smelling during parent teacher meetings."

Allie had a list of each of the teachers that worked at the school. Even when the others started taking notes on what she was saying, she was still nervous. Looking up at Clarkson when she finished with her list, she smiled at him.

"This is the plan that you are all going to follow. Each

of you owns twenty percent of the school. You're going to each sell me half of what you have. Clarkson? You're going to sell me eleven percent of what you have. Now." He told her he was off her rocker. "Am I? No. I don't think so. What I am is a great deal smarter than you are. Not only that, but I have resources that will put you all behind bars. As part owners of this sham of a school, you're going to be held as responsible as he is. So how much do you want for your shares?"

"You're not getting shit from any of us. No one can sell their shares unless it's approved by all of us. And I'm not budging." Allie asked him if he was sure. "You bet your sweet little ass, I'm sure. This has been a moneymaker since we started it. I'm not going to have some little twit come in here and start telling us what you want to do. Nor will I put any of the money back in the school. It's working out just fine for me."

"What about us?" She had to think who this woman was when she turned and smiled at her. "Issa Johnson, Allie. I want it on the record that I had no idea about the teachers or the money being taken from the school. That's no excuse, but I'd like to know how that money he has wasn't shared with the rest of us. Not that I would have taken it if I knew what was going on, but he's been stealing all along from every one of us."

"That's very true. I'd like the same question answered. Why haven't you told us what you're doing? Like Issa, I don't want the money, but knowing that you have taken it all without our approval is something I had no idea about either." Mr. Cable told her his name. "Also, I'd like for Allie here to answer how much money he stole from us."

"Since, as I said, its inception, he's taken just over six million dollars in cash, and another three million in things such as houses, a few boats, and lavish vacations that he takes his mistress on, and not his wife and children." The information was being fed to her from Beck. She supposed he was getting it from the others. The other women were helping but leaving her alone to her tasks. "You might also want to know that there are four million dollars in insurance claims that he's made on your behalf. When a student or teacher is harmed, he is keeping that money for himself. The teachers say nothing about the hospital charging them when there was a claim because they haven't any idea that he's doing it. He's — pardon my language, but he's fucking you guys all the way around."

"You lie." She told Clarkson she didn't. And she could get them proof should they want it. The other four members said that they did. "I'm betting it's all fabricated. She's in with the other Robinsons. They'll steal from anyone if they think they can make a buck."

"That doesn't make any sense. If I was stealing from someone, I'd be making money. Moron. So, lady and gentlemen, are you going to sell me your shares or not?" Clarkson again said that he wasn't, so they weren't. "If you say so. I have my husband here. He has a few things he wants to show you as well."

Going to the door, she had to pause for a second

or two to breathe. This was going to be the scary part. Someone could seriously be hurt. Opening the door, she winked at Beck before he allowed his cat to take him. When he moved into the room, he leaped up onto the conference table and walked along it to Clarkson. They were forehead to forehead, and she thought it was the best thing that could have happened today. The man started screaming right away.

"Enough." When one of them stood up, Allie cautioned them. "If you run, he'll chase you. All cats — and Beck here is no exception — will chase you down and think you're his new play toy. Don't run or make any sudden moves, or he'll hurt you. Now. As I was saying, you're going to sell me half of your shares, or else. I'm going to let that dangle out there for a moment while my husband here shows you his paw. It's quite impressive, isn't it? Now, darling, show them your claws."

"I don't want anything to do with this place after today." Mrs. Johnson smiled at her. "I think that once you and your family gets ahold of this place, not only will it be a wonderful place to work, but it will also be the safest one around. I'm donating my shares to you because I think this place will only improve with you and your family at the helm."

"We'll pay you for the shares, Mrs. Johnson." Shaking her head, Mrs. Johnson pulled her shares out of a file that she had brought in with her and signed her name to them. "Thank you for this. I promise you, this will be a safe place for all people."

"I'm going to call my attorney right now. There is a fax machine in this office. I'll have him send you a copy of my shares as well. I find myself no longer wanting to be a part of something so terribly wrong. That gives you forty shares." Mr. Cable turned to the man on his right, Mr. Parker, who was the only person who'd not spoken. "What do you think Margaret would say if she knew this was what her money was being used for, Alford? I would bet right now she's rolling over in her grave. Margaret would be coming here right away if she knew what this bastard has done to her school."

"She would at that. I was just seeing how I could get my attorney to come on down here and turn mine over to her as well. What are you going to do, Patrick Gibson? I know we have the same attorney. Should I have him bring yours down as well?" Gibson said to do it. Mr. Parker looked at Clarkson. Beck was still staring at him. "If I were you, Ben, I'd give it up. She's got all she needs now to run you out of town. And if she doesn't, well then, I guess it's been nice knowing you. Mrs. Robinson, is this really Beckett?"

"Yes. My husband." The man scratched Beck behind the ear. "I don't think he knew you were on this board, Mr. Parker. He said he would have done this differently if he had."

"Nope. The way you two did this is the perfect way to have brought us down. If you'd not mind, with a full background check, if you will, I'd like to be on some of the committees that the Robinsons will have installed here. You're part of a good family, ma'am. In the event you've not figured that out as yet."

"I have. Thank you for your help." He said it was his pleasure. As he left the room with Mrs. Johnson, Mr. Gibson wasn't far behind, going out with Mr. Cable. She now had eighty shares of the school — more than enough to fire Clarkson. "Well, well, well, Clarkson. It looks as if you're the only holdout. Not that it matters one hill of beans. The Robinson Foundation owns more than enough to get you fired."

"You can't fire me, you little twit. I started this project and intend to get as much out of it as I can. There won't be any stopping me either. I know for a fact that this room has a recording in it. It's how I kept the others in line. You see, you have nothing. It's your word against mine about what transpired today." The phone in the middle of the conference table rang, startling all three of them, including Beck. "Answer that. I'm sure it's one of my people saying they've changed their minds."

"Hello, fucktard. My name is Rogen Robinson. I wanted you to know that as of ten minutes ago, I've not only emptied your bank accounts but also that your home is being gone over by some very smart people. You won't be able to stay there, I'm afraid. They're going to be taking whatever they want and going over it." Clarkson asked Rogen what she thought she was going to find. "Find? We've already found a great deal of things, as a matter of fact. Not just the bank money, which, as I said, we've taken, but also your porn. While it's not your run of the mill sort of porn, I wonder if you realize that having porn on a computer that you've told the IRS is only used for work is wrong. Also, and this I find so funny I nearly wet myself, they've found the ad that you put into newspapers all over the country to hire sex offenders for the school that you no longer work at. I think it's safe to say that you're going to be gone for a very long time."

The Feds didn't say a word to Allie or Clarkson as they gathered him up with the computer and other electronic devices in the room. No one even commented on the fact that there was a large tiger stretched out like a tiger rug on the table. After they were gone, the room silent except for their breathing, Allie looked at Beck. He yawned hugely, and she burst out laughing.

"I'm sorry. Did I take you from your nap time, Beck? Or does this sort of thing happen to you so much that you find it boring as fuck?" He told her he loved her and was very proud of her. "That didn't answer my question, but it was a good save. Do you think Tru will be all right with how we did this?"

"I fucking love you, girl. Christ, that was epic." Allie had forgotten about the phone, and it still being on. Tru laughed as she continued. "I nearly shit myself when Beck walked along that table. Holy fuck balls. That was great. I'm so happy right now that I could fire off my gun until it just snapped that it was empty. Wonderful job, Allie. Your plan was perfect. And I have to admit, your way not only got us the school that we can work with, but it also made us some very important friends in the process. We've already gotten calls from three of the attorneys of the people there that are pledging their support to any way we reopen the school. They're also volunteering to testify against Clarkson and to help us in any way they can to make sure nothing like this happens again."

"I didn't expect them to donate the shares to us."

Tru said that was what made it so important. They didn't have to pay anyone for them, so it didn't look like they had taken anything from them in the way of a bribe. Not that any of that mattered. "Each of the people there today have signed off on their paperwork before they left the office. You did good."

"We all did well today." They were laughing and hooting around the phone, and Allie stood up. "I think I'm going to gather up my family and go out to eat. This has been a terribly stressful few days for me." Anna told her that she was there now and she was glad for her.

"Good job today, Allie. I just heard. Why don't just you and Beck go out? I'll keep the kids." She told Anna that it was too much on her. "It's not really. They love the babies, and it wears them out when they have someone to play with. Even Eddie enjoys having them around."

It was a date then. She and Beck would be going out on their first date. Laughing, she told him what she was thinking. When he shifted back to his manly self, she realized how lucky she was to have such a wonderful family in her corner.

Chapter 8

Holly wasn't sure what she was supposed to do with the kids on the floor with her. Conor had gone off with Mr. Morgan to look over some things that he was working on. She hadn't wanted to go, so she was there now with three babies crawling all over her.

"Can you tell them apart? The girls, I mean?" Holly told Anna who she thought they were. "Good. Morgan still messes them up sometimes. But he loves them to pieces. You seem very unsure of yourself right now."

"I haven't been around babies before. They're very clingy, aren't they?" Anna laughed and told her they would be until they could walk. They were using her as a hand up. "They don't know how to walk?"

"No. They're very close, but they are still holding onto things when they move around. Marie is the most adventurous, but she is also the one that is taking her time in learning that she can let go. I think since Renee hurt her head the other day when she let go of the chair, she's decided that she's not taking the chance of her head getting bumped." Holly thought that their mom was wrong, that they could walk, but didn't say anything. "Eddie has a long way to go yet. He's watching his sisters get around, and I think he's jealous."

"When they start walking, do you think they'll show him how to do it?" Anna told her that was probably what was going to happen. "Grandpa Robinson said that the cycle of a person is round. That you start out not knowing anything until you learn a few things. Then as you grow older, you start to reverse yourself and don't know anything again. I think that's just sad."

"He's been thinking about his death a great deal lately. Like he's going to go to bed every night and not wake up. I've been talking to him about it, but he's a stubborn old goat." Marie came to stand on her lap. She didn't weigh much, but it was still a little scary to have her there. "They won't break, Holly. They just love people."

"I know. Renee was standing on her sister a few minutes ago, and I thought for sure they were going to have a rumble." They both laughed. "I'd like to show you something. If you don't mind."

"No. Go ahead." Holly put Renee by the other couch, then she did the same for Marie. "They'll be dropping down to their butts in a minute to get to you—"

Marie took her sister's hand, and the two of them walked across the room toward her. They had to stop a couple of times to steady themselves, but they made it all the way to her. When she and Anna clapped, all three of the kids clapped as well.

"You got them to walk to you!" Anna said that she wanted to see if they could do it again. "That way, I can record it. Oh, Holly, you got them to do something none of us have been able to do. They're walking."

"They will come to me one at a time, but they'd rather be holding hands. I think if we were to put something in their hands as they walked over here, they'd do it on their own. Marie might not need anything, but Renee does." She put the girls back by the other couch and handed Renee the stuffed tiger that was on the floor. "Come on, guys. Show Mommy how smart you are."

They did it again, this time not holding hands but having fun—every few steps, they'd have to stop and clap their hands. By the time they were halfway to her, Renee had dropped the stuffed animal and made her way to her on her own. It was the greatest thing she'd ever witnessed.

"I can't believe it. They're walking." The girls were so happy with themselves that they walked to Anna. Holly wasn't sure what was going on when Anna started crying. She told her she was sorry. "No. You didn't do anything wrong, Holly. I'm just happy. So happy that you did this for us. There's not going to be anything to stop them now. Have you done anything else since you've been here? I'm betting if you hung around more, they'd be going to college next week. I'm joking. I'm so happy right now."

Eddie could sit up, but he was like a little toy. Once he got too excited or even moved too much, he'd roll right over onto his back again. Holly would set him up so that he could try it again.

The girls, pleased with the hand claps and people gushing over them, were all over the living room now. They would fall a few times and had to be helped up, but Anna was right; there was no stopping them now. Also, she noticed that everything within their reach was fair game to them. The room was such a mess that Holly started picking things up. Renee knocked her brother over, trying to knock some of the pretty things off the coffee table, and Holly scolded her.

It broke her heart when Renee's lower lip came out and quivered a little. Then big fat tears started to fall before she wailed like Holly had hit her. Anna said to not get caught up in her scheme for getting away with something, but it hurt Holly too much not to cuddle the little girl.

"I'm sorry I hurt your heart, Renee. But you have to be careful of your brother. He's littler than you." The little girl looked up at her, still crying tears that made her own eyes fill with them. "When I was a little girl, the little boy across the street was forever hurting my feelings too. He was older than Conor and me, so neither of us wanted to tell on him. Besides, his mommy and daddy weren't nice anyway. They said that they had raised him right. Perhaps it was just us that was making him lash out. One day Conor and I were waiting at the ice cream truck for our turn. Billy, that was his name, watched us. I knew he was going to try and take our treats. So you know what we did? We bought him a treat as well. When he came toward us to do his nastiest, Conor handed him the cone we'd bought, and we walked away. He was a little bit nicer to us after that. Not all the time, but he wasn't as mean." She looked at Anna. "I have no idea why I told her that. It just came out."

"You comforted her with your story. Not the words, but that you were talking to her in a calm voice. Look, she's ready to fall asleep now." She was too. Blinking longer and longer until she just left her eyes closed. "You and your brother haven't had an easy life, have you?"

"I don't think we were as bad as some families were. The homes they put us in when we lived at the foster place were terrible places, but it wasn't so bad since we were together. But the people were getting meaner about things as we kept failing to be a family with them." Anna told her it wasn't them. "I guess I sort of know that too. When those people tied me to the bed, all I could think about was that I was going to die. I closed off my mind to what was going to happen and thought of something that Conor and I had done that was fun. Conor saved me. He was hurt, but he told me he'd die for me. Beck and Allie, they're nothing like the others, are they?"

"No. They'd die for you as well. You understand that, don't you?" Holly said she didn't know. "Trust me when I tell you, honey, they'd do anything in the world to save you from harm."

"Conor gets into trouble a lot. Not as much as he used to when we first moved in with them, but he said that he hates them sometimes. Like I said, not so much as he did the first day or two. Then he tells me that he loves them too. I do like them a great deal, but they scare me. Not them, I guess, but that they could turn us back over to the home. Conor said he's feeling that too. Like they're just waiting for us to be happy, then they'll take it away from us."

"I know you have no reason to believe me, but they're never going to get rid of the two of you. Ever. They've fallen in love with you." Holly said that she heard Allie crying sometimes. "Have you asked her why?"

"No. I'm not sure how to ask her." Holly looked at the baby sleeping in her arms. "I've been thinking that as soon as they have their own kids, they'll not want us anymore. I mean, you have three babies here. Would you adopt another one and treat them the same?"

"Holly, these three babies aren't of my body. I didn't give birth to them. But they're mine the same as if I had. I love them that much. But they're adopted the same as you and your brother, as well as Jimmy." That shocked her. No one treated them like they were castoffs, and she told Anna that. "Castoffs? I can only assume that someone called you that. Well, it's not true. All of us, the entire family, is waiting on the two of you to show that you want to be a part of the Robinson family. We all feel like you don't want to be a part of us."

Holly thought about that, what Anna said when she

went to get on the computer for Rogen. Was it their fault that the others treated them differently? She knew she was trying her best not to get close to them. That way, it wouldn't hurt so much when they were sent away. She'd done that before, gotten attached to the dog that the Hendersons had, and it had hurt her badly when they were taken from the little mutt.

These weren't dogs, however. They were real people. People that had made sure she and her brother had everything and anything that they needed. Even Conor had himself a job, picking up the sticks that had fallen out of the trees last week. It wasn't even a *just do it* job, he told her. He was getting paid real money and not just promised. The Robinsons told him that picking up the sticks and piling them up meant that an animal or two could either use the pile in the winter months or take some of them to his home to make it stronger.

"Beck said that the entire ecosystem depends on all of us doing our part so that everything in the next part will have what they need to make the next part of the circle work. I never knew that so much depended on me just picking up sticks in the yard, did you?" Holly had told him that she'd read it once in a book. "I'm learning so much from Beck and Allie. I hope we get to stay long enough that we can learn more stuff."

It hadn't occurred to either of them that this would be long term. That they could be there forever, as Allie had been telling her. Neither Allie nor Beck included them in things just to make themselves look good, but they asked them what they wanted to do. Like today.

When Anna joined her again, Renee was awake and jabbering to her sister. Eddie was joining them some, and Holly thought it was adorable. She still couldn't believe these kids weren't Anna's real kids. No one seemed to care.

"I don't know what to do about this." Anna asked her what she wanted to do. "Be in this family. To be able to stay here forever. I don't want to leave here, ever. I like having food all the time when I want it. And a warm bed. Last night, it was so wonderful to be able to get into bed and know that no one would bother me there. That I could even, if I wanted, stay up later so long as I knew I'd have to get up early for school. No one has ever done things like that for us."

"Do you want to stay with them for the things they do for you, Holly? It's all right if that's what you want. But I hope you'll also open your heart to love us as much as we already do you." Holly asked her if she really loved her. "Yes. Of course. You're a very sweet girl. You've been hurt; I understand that too. But no one here will harm you in anyway."

"They said that they'd die for me." Anna told her that was right. "I don't think my parents would have done that for me—I know they wouldn't have. No one would have before coming here. They only wanted us around for the money, I think."

"More than likely, that is most of it. You two have been through hell and back. I can't believe how lucky you were to have survived. And you did too. Survive when all the odds were against you. Now, look where you are. With a couple that loves you, a family that loves to have you around and enjoys your company. Even the kids all love you." She looked at the girls playing with the blocks she'd gotten out for them. "If you keep this up, keeping a good eye on the kids, you'll have no end of babysitting jobs. I do hope you know I'm paying you for this. It's been wonderful for me to just be able to come and go without worrying about what they might get into."

"I don't— They're my cousins, aren't they?" Anna laughed and said that they were. "So are the other kids. They're my cousins, and you're my aunt."

"I am. So does that mean you're going to open up a little with us, young lady?" Getting up, she made her way to Anna. Hugging her tightly, holding onto her with just the knowledge that she could, Holly felt her eyes fill with tears again. "Oh, Holly. I have wanted to say this to you and Conor so much. I love you, sweetie. So much. And welcome to the family."

She was part of a family. Not only that, but she had a family too. Her heart felt as full as it had ever felt. When she sat back down on the floor, all she could think about was that she had a forever home. That she could love them and not have to worry about being broken-hearted when they had to move on. Because no one was going to make them move on.

Anna had another call, and when she left, Holly picked up her cell phone. That was something else that she and her brother had gotten. Phones that were theirs forever too. The word forever was taking on an entirely new meaning for her.

It took Holly five minutes of playing with the babies and finding the right emoji that she wanted to use. Setting up a text, her first text, she told Beck and Allie that she loved them. And that she wanted to be their forever daughter. Hitting send was the hardest thing she'd done. Holding her breath, she only hoped that they'd send her something back that would —

Her phone rang, and Allie's face appeared. Answering it, Holly just knew that she was going to tell her not to text such nonsense to them again. But the excitement in her voice had Holly thinking they'd be making fun of her.

"I love you too, Holly. Beck is driving, but he said to tell you that he loves you and Conor so very much that he's glad he gets to say that back to you. Oh, honey. We are so happy that you love us. We love you." Allie laughed, and so did she. "You have no idea how happy you've made us just now. Thank you for letting us know. I will treasure this text message forever. I love you so much."

When she ended the call a few minutes later, Holly felt on top of the world. When Conor came in, she told him what she and Anna had spoken about. Then she told him what she'd done by texting Allie and Beck. He asked her what they'd said.

"That they love me too." Conor nodded and told

her he wasn't sure. "That's okay, I think. You'll fall in love with them on your own. I just needed to say that to them. Conor, we have cousins. Aunts and uncles. Grandparents. Nobody has ever given that to us before. Do you realize that we have so much right now that I'm about to bust with happiness?"

"I can tell." He watched the babies with her, playing with them when they walked toward him. "I don't know yet. I don't want to love them, then have to tell them that I don't. Morgan told me that he loved me a bit ago. It felt really good." She told him it should. "I'll think about it, okay?"

"Of course you can." She giggled. "Conor, these kids, they're adopted. Did you know that? All the kids so far have been adopted. I think that's wonderful."

He seemed shocked about it like she had been, but he didn't say anything. Holly knew he'd come around. And when he did, he'd feel as good about it as she did. Being with the Robinsons had been everything she used to dream of in being a part of a family. And more, she realized. They were more than she could have hoped for.

~*~

It was strange to be out on a date with a man that she already loved. Allie was so happy right now that she wanted to race home and make sure Holly hadn't changed her mind about how she felt about them. Beck asked her if she was still thinking about Holly.

"I am. It's a great feeling to think that a person you've already fallen in love with loves you back." He said that he loved her. "And I love you. But these kids— Holly, I'm sure it was difficult for her to say that. Anna told me they're afraid to get attached. They don't want to get heartbroken when we send them back. I'd never do that, but I do understand why they'd feel that way."

"I do too. I can't believe how lucky we are to have them with us. And having family around them is something I don't think they've had a lot of. Morgan was showing Conor around the barn and the things he'd thought of as manly. He said that he seemed bored until he let him ride the lawnmower around the yard. That was when it occurred to me that he'd be driving in a couple of years." They both laughed as they were being seated. "I've never eaten here before, but Rogen told me they're wonderful. I have to thank her for getting us a reservation."

The place was packed. Allie didn't want to know what she'd had to do to get them a table. Rogen had told her that the Chicken Lombardy was her favorite thing on the menu. Allie tried not to be shocked by the prices. She looked up at Beck when he said her name.

"It's fine, you know. We can afford this and more if you want." She nodded. "No, don't just do that. I would never lie to you. We have money, the two of us. A great deal of it that we can spend however we want. Both of us have good jobs too, so it's not like we're just living off what we have. I promise you, love, we have plenty enough for this dinner."

"I'm trying to get that 'not looking at the price tag' mentality that Rogen told me I need to adapt to. She said that even if we didn't have a considerable bank account, we still have money elsewhere." He said that was right. "I know. But after having nothing my entire life, suddenly having it takes a little getting used to."

"I can imagine that. I know you won't go crazy with spending money, and it is good to look at a price tag, but I can understand what she means." Allie said she could as well. "So, get whatever you want from the menu, and then maybe, after, you might get lucky."

"You know I've been lucky several times a day, don't you? There are times when I swear to you I think you go out and drink some magical potion that makes you want me again." He told her it was only his love for her. "Thank you. That was sweet. I love you."

Dinner was wonderful. Not only did they try several appetizers, but they also shared three meals. Being tigers made them both hungry more often, as well as making their appetites bigger. It made for some strange looks at times, but that was something else she was getting used to. Ignoring people and their looking at her.

After dinner, they walked around the town. Window shopping with someone was a good deal more fun than shopping alone. As usual, their conversation steered back to the kids and how much they wanted them both to be happy with them.

Her cell was ringing just as they were getting an ice cream cone at the creamery. It was Rogen.

"I know you didn't want to be disturbed tonight, but I knew you'd want this news. When the police went to talk to Mr. Grant and look at his car, he confessed. Not only had he hit the boy, but he had dragged him to his parents' driveway after he'd done it. I guess he couldn't get anyone to fix his car because it had blood on it." Allie asked her what would happen now. "I would imagine that you pick up more work now that word is out that you can find murderers with nothing more than a police report. I'm very proud of you. That really was a good find for you."

"I had Beck with me, so he gets some credit too." She laughed, and Rogen snorted. "I do have two more that I'm working on now. It's sort of fun, I have to admit. To take a crime scene and make it more real. Thank you for all the stuff to make it work."

"It has helped us all out. Now the police department in Nevada owes us one. Not that I didn't charge them for the job you did for them, but also, they'll remember this was a solid circumstance of where a case was closed. You did good, my dear, and we're making connections on an entirely new level for us to tap into." Allie told her she thought that would help. "It does. All right. I'll let you go. I do hope he's taking good care of you. You're much too stressed all the time as it is."

"That put a feather in your cap, I'm thinking." She nodded at Beck as they had their treat. "I hate to bring this up now, but I have another trip next week. I don't know how long it will take me to get it taken care of, but at least a week. Will you be all right?"

"Yes. If you mean with the kids, then double yes. I'm

having so much fun being a mom to them." Beck told her he could tell. "Good. Also, I think your dad has a trip in mind for them to take with him. I don't have all the details, but then I trust him as much as I do you."

"Thank you. My dad is planning to take them on a whole day fishing trip. He's hoping they enjoy it so much that they'll want to keep doing it with him." Allie told him she'd never been. "Apparently, neither have the kids. But it might not be a complete wash for him. Dad would fish every day if he could. Mom would kill him, simply because he is that good at it. But she'd have to get a bigger freezer if he were to catch more than they could eat."

"I wouldn't even know how to take a fish off the hook, much less catch one. But I do love fresh fish. It has a taste so much different than the frozen stuff that I could have it daily. Okay, not daily, but perhaps every other day."

Beck told her about the one and only fishing trip that Dad had taken all of them on. "He was either baiting hooks, taking them out of one of us, or keeping us from tipping the boat. When I look back on that, it's a small wonder that he didn't drown us all. Mom would have been upset, but Dad, we really put him through a hard time that day." Beck laughed. "I don't think we caught a single fish. Thatcher ended up getting three hooks in his head. I think Dawson got soaked twice when we tipped the boat. I really think we should try it again with Dad. Do you think he'd take us?"

"Doubtful. It sounds to me like you made him not want to do anything with the six of you at once ever again—your poor dad. I can see him, too, getting frustrated with you guys. Trying hard to be patient with you." She laughed. "I do think your mom would have enjoyed you guys taking more trips with your father. I doubt there was ever any peace for her when you guys were all home."

"No. And even when we started to leave home, she still had to contend with us. One of us would need her help with something or another. Most of the time, it was how to cook something, or even for us to come by with a laundry issue. Mom taught us all how to take care of things like that, but an odd thing would pop up unexpectantly."

Allie listened to all his stories about his parents and family. The Robinsons, a family that she loved being a part of, seemed to get along better than most families. She didn't think it was wholly due to them being cats, either. They just loved each other that much. And that hard. Even the in-laws, the other women, loved as they did.

When they made their way back home, she realized how exhausted she was. There were several messages on her service, nothing that she was going to deal with tonight. Even Beck had a few of his own that he left for tomorrow.

"I'm thinking before it gets too much later in the year, we should decide if we're going to put in an outbuilding for the lawn things or just store it in the barn that we have now." She asked him why he thought of that now. "I have no idea. I was just thinking that we might want to invest in a larger barn so the kids can store their cars in there. Just now, it occurred to me that they'll have to not want to drive for us to be storing their cars. I never went anywhere that didn't involve me driving when I got my first car."

"Your mom told me that you all had to pay half for your first cars." He said that was right. "Then, since it worked out so well for you guys, I see no reason to make our kids do anything less. I know that Conor has a job now, and Holly will have one when she's old enough. Anna did mention to me tonight that she thought that Holly was responsible enough to babysit for the family."

"I thought she'd enjoy the kids." Allie thought of the message she'd gotten from Holly and nearly cried again. "Don't be getting all mushy with me, my love. I don't think I can handle your tears tonight. I love you so very much."

Even as her head hit the pillow, her last thoughts were on the kids. She let her mind go over the events of having them there and was thrilled beyond words that they'd taken them in. Rolling to her side to snuggle with Beck, she wondered what the next fifty or so years would bring the two of them.

Chapter 9

Dawson looked over the file that had come in with the newest patient. She'd passed away not an hour ago, her injuries just too much with the blood loss she'd sustained. He wanted to figure out who he was supposed to notify, and there just wasn't enough information in the thing to tell him if she even had next of kin. He heard someone coming toward him as he closed the file. It was Agent Fry.

"I can take it from here for you, Doctor. I'm sorry I wasn't here sooner." He said he'd been able to handle it. "I'm sure you have been. You and Doctor Thatcher have saved more than we've been able to before this place opened. It's nice for the rest of us to know that there is someone out there that will care for us like we're someone important."

"You all are. Every life is." She nodded at him like she didn't believe that line anymore than he did. "All right, most every life is important. The lowlife you guys brought in here the other day has had me second guessing everything I worked for in becoming a doctor. Why was he brought here, anyway? I thought this was just for agents."

"He's giving us information that we can use to close up a lot of loose ends. Mr. J will end up in prison when we've gotten all we can from him. Right now, he needs to be healthy so we can get it. You did all right. I know for a fact that it was touch and go there for a few minutes when he called you a fucking hack, but you got over it and helped him to mend." She laughed. "I might well have ended him myself the way he was treating my agents."

Agent Fry had been their go to person since the clinic had opened. She made sure that the paperwork was filled out correctly and filed away in the room that held as many files as he'd bet the largest library did books. He'd not been in there but the one time, and that was enough for him to know he wanted no part of it. The place was guarded by armed people that wore only black and carried large guns. Also, the rooms were fireproof as well as protected against any other major disaster that might hit, including a direct hit with a bomb. Yes, he stayed the hell out of there.

Since they'd been working the clinic, he and Thatcher had lost three patients—one agent, and the other two just people in their town. It was strange having to keep the place he was in now private. He'd bet his last paycheck from the government that not one person would believe him if he were to talk about what they did in here. Not that he ever would.

The pay was amazing, too, more than triple what he'd been making when he'd been a partner in a firm. As they also paid his malpractice insurance as well as his health, he was able to put away even more than he'd ever been able to before. His home was paid for. A new car was his every year, he'd been told, and since he was working for the government, his home was furnished with the best equipment and staff. They took care of their own very well.

Thatcher was in his office when he got back to his own. "Hey, do you have a couple of minutes?" Dawson told him he had lots of time, as it was only a half-day for them. "I really needed this half-day today too. Christ, it's been a strange few weeks. Do you remember that man? His name was Carlos or something like that? He'd been in here for an infected splinter. Do you know who I'm talking about?"

"Not Carlos, but Theos." Thatcher said that was it. "Yes. He even did his follow up last week as you told him to do. What's up? Did he skip out on the bill or something?"

"No. I don't know, actually. But I just got a phone call from his wife—or so she said. But he's going to lose a leg from my work." Dawson sat down on the other seat in Thatcher's office and asked him what was going on. "I honestly have no idea. I'm not even sure I believe he's hurting that badly. I know that sounds crazy, but all we did was remove a splinter. Even at his check up, it was scarred over and healed."

"Is she blaming you?" Thatcher nodded. "Have you called it in? I mean, that's what we were told to do when we get calls like that. I do understand you being confused, but let the insurance handle it."

"I did call it in. Then they called me back and told me that there wasn't anyone alive by the name, and the social that I gave them was for a dead person. That's why I asked you if you remembered him. Just in case I got it wrong." Thatcher handed him the file that was marked, outpatient. "Apparently, even the address they gave was bogus. I told the agency that I had called it in as he wasn't anyone that I knew, but now they want me to give Rogen not only the file but anything I might have kept with his DNA on it. I'm glad they have us take a DNA test from everyone that comes in here. Christ, this is a nightmare."

"Rogen say anything? I mean, like this was stupid or something?" Thatcher said that all she said was that the agency was looking into it. "What if they don't believe you? Do you think they'll have Rogen take you out?"

"Like I'd do that. Don't let your asses get ahead of the big picture." Rogen joined them in the room and kissed Thatcher on the mouth. "I just got a call from the shitholes that have you thinking I'd take you out. I love you guys too much for me to do that on my own. I'd hire someone. The DNA matches one of the agents that has had his employment ended."

"Do I want to know what that means?" Rogen just

smiled at him. "All right. I don't want to know. But what happens now? I mean, are we going to be shut down or something? Did we do anything wrong? I have to tell you, Rogen, I'm enjoying this life of making good money. I was just thinking about how much I love the perks too."

"Not that I can see from what they've asked about the two of you. He was never beyond the point of no return. He didn't stay overnight, nor did his wife, who he isn't married to, make it back to the room with him. I'd say you did just what you were told to do." Thatcher asked her what happened now. "I have to send Tru out."

That meant the man was as good as dead. So was the woman. He wanted to ask why they had jumped to that point but decided he wasn't really sure he wanted to know. When she sat on the edge of the desk, Dawson was sure he was going to be shot as well.

"You should never play poker, Dawson. It's written all over your face that you're thinking I'm going to hurt you in some way. I'm not." She did take her gun out, and Dawson finally understood the terminology that people used when their ass puckered tight, and their balls felt like they were going to crawl up there inside of his ass. "Dawson. Breathe, damn it. I'm going to have you carry this from now on. Thatcher is already armed, but you need to be too."

"No. I don't like guns." Rogen asked him if he thought he'd enjoy dying more. "No. But seriously, with all this firepower around here all the time, who would be stupid enough to try and hurt us?"

"He got into your clinic, didn't he?" There was that. Taking the gun from her, he laid it on his lap. "You also need to get more practice with that thing. I know you've qualified to use it, but I really need you to feel like if push came to shove, you'd know it's going to save your life. You can go with your parents. They go down to the shooting range twice a week. Unlike you, they're armed all the time."

"You have no idea how much I hate the thought of having to use this. But I can see your point in knowing how. I'll go there tomorrow. I promise." Putting it in his back pocket, for now, he started out the door. Rogen called him back. "I'm carrying it. What now, my dear?"

"You'll need this." She helped him put on the under the arm holster. It wasn't nearly as cumbersome as he thought it might be. "Wear it, Dawson. If I find your dead body someplace and you've not at least pulled that thing to defend yourself, I'm going to have you brought back to life so I can kill you myself."

Dawson nodded and walked to his own office. The thing was, he believed her. That not only would she figure out how to bring him back, but that she would indeed kill him again. And not quickly, either.

As he entered his office, he closed the door behind him. He sat at his desk and thought about what had happened last night. Now that had been a scary ending of a day.

He and Jonas had been out just fooling around. They'd hit a bar at some point. While neither of them were drunk, they had a nice buzz from the beers. As they were leaving the little diner that was open twenty-four/ seven, a woman approached them. She pulled a knife on them and demanded their money.

Dawson reached into his pocket to pull out his wallet. Jonas just stood there. When she told him to hurry it up, Jonas said that he'd worked hard for his money, and he wasn't turning it over to anyone. Dawson thought for sure that they were both going to be killed.

"You fucking moron, Jonas. What the hell are you thinking?" He looked at his brother when the woman said his name. "You're supposed to give me your money because you owe me support."

"I don't owe you shit, Margo. You're a junkie and a whore. Literally. I told you the last time that I wasn't going to help you out anymore. You get straight, and I'll make sure you're put up so you can get your kids back. But as it stands right now, you're fucked." She stomped her foot, and Jonas laughed. "You don't scare me one bit. Now, move along before I have to call in a few favors and make sure you never get your kids back."

"I fucking hate you." Jonas told her he didn't care all that much for her either. "You mother fucker. I should just kill you both right now."

Jonas reached out and snatched the knife from her. It scared Dawson so much that he jumped back. When his brother bent the knife in two and snapped it, Dawson wondered what she'd do now.

"Go home, Margo. And barring that, you should just

go back to the rock you crawled out from under. You and I are done. I'm not going to help you again." She begged him to give her another chance. "No. Go away before I get pissed off and shift. You know that my cat will hurt you if he doesn't kill you."

They were nearly a street away when he finally asked Jonas what that was all about. If anyone had asked him to describe his brother, he would have said he was a nerd. A numbers guy who could take a buck and have a million in no time. Not this stranger that grabbed knives from crazy women and walked away.

"She met up with me about six months ago. To *borrow* some money. I didn't give her anything but the phone number of some people to get her straightened out. That ended badly, as she never even tried, and the courts ended up taking her kids from her. She has four." Dawson asked him why she said he owed her. "Margo is messed up in the head. She seems to think that just because I recommended her getting clean, I had something to do with her kids being taken. They were malnourished. Underweight, as you can imagine, as well as the little one was suffering from a very severe case of diaper rash because there was never any diapers for the others to change her when she needed it. You should have seen them, Dawson. They were terrified that their mother was coming back to move them along again."

"What did you do with them? I have no idea why, but I have a feeling you've stashed them someplace that she'll not ever get them no matter how clean she is." Jonas told him he had and for him to leave it at that. "I will. However, if you'd like me to look them over or anything, just let me know. I won't tell a soul. I promise."

"I might take you up on that. But for now, they're safe, clean, and being fed well." They didn't mention it again, but he was afraid for his brother. The woman obviously knew that Jonas was a cat, but she had jumped him anyway. "It's all right, Dawson. I've been dealing with this sort of person for some time now."

"You really do, don't you? I mean, if anyone would have asked me, I'd have said you were afraid of your own shadow. But tonight? Well, you startled me into realizing that you're very badassed, aren't you?" Jonas said he'd not go that far. "However you want to see yourself, I see a man who is not afraid of danger and is willing to go out on a limb for someone. Are the children really safe? The reason I ask is, Margo looked unhinged."

"She is. And I mean that in the worst sort of way. But the kids are safe. If they weren't, I would ask for help. I'm not stupid enough to think I'm invincible." Dawson was glad to hear that. "I'll see what I can arrange for you to see them. I believe they're all healthy. But there might be something I don't know that you'd see. But don't tell anyone, Dawson. I like having people think I'm just a laid back numbers man."

For the rest of the night, and well into the morning after getting home, Dawson had had his phone close to his side. Every noise he'd heard, it was his brother asking for help. Just as the sun was coming up, he realized how stupid he was being.

Obviously, Jonas had been doing this for a while now and hadn't had any trouble. Why did Dawson think that because he knew it would turn to shit? Dawson turned his calls over to the service, with strict instructions to make sure they called him if one of his brothers called, and went to sleep. He was, of course, late to work, and that set the tone for his entire day today. Running behind was never a good thing for him.

~*~

Tru slipped in through the door and sat at the bar. It was a nice place. Full of people, just the way she liked it, and her target was over at the pool table having a good time, it appeared. He wasn't playing, but he was loud with his insults to the other players. She sipped her glass of wine and waited on the other person she was here to end.

It had never been a problem for her to end the lives of people on her list, not even now that she had a family of her own. She told herself that if she didn't take care of them, they might someday be after her or her family.

Just as she was pushing away her glass to be refilled, the woman walked into the bar.

"Christ." She smiled at the bartender when he shook his head at the other woman. He was pouring another glass for her. "You'd think they'd at least take a look in the mirror before leaving their room, wouldn't you? I mean, where did she get that outfit? Hookers are Us or something? It's not just too small, but it doesn't leave much to the imagination, now does it?"

"Some people don't care." He told her he surely wished they did. "I agree with you there. The notion that one size fits all has gotten out of hand. I noticed now the label says one size fits most. It's the most that I worry about."

She didn't mind making small talk with the bartender. Tru had always believed they knew more than anyone in the place. If she wanted intel, she went to a bar. If she wanted to find the best place to eat, the bartender would always steer her in the right direction. Best hotel. Best show. They would have the knowledge that would mean you'd have a wonderful time.

They were also the most closed-mouth people on the planet. The police knew better than to ask them questions. A bar wouldn't be open long if the owner talked trash about his clients. His staff would be just as closed-mouth unless it was a murder or robbery of himself or his personnel. Then they'd only give them the details involving that. Tru had been able to hide behind a bar when some shit came in shooting. She loved the people that ran bars almost as she did doctors.

When the woman went to the bathroom, Tru didn't immediately follow her. She knew that she and the man would go out to smoke at some point in the night. That was where she was going to take them both. It was quick and quiet. When the female came out of the bathroom, Tru sat very still. This wasn't her usual way of doing her business.

"Charlie, there ain't any paper in the ladies' room." Perfect, Tru thought and got up to go into the bathroom herself. Just as she was passing the female, she told her the same thing she told Charlie. "He'll just hand it over, and I can slip it under the door for you, honey."

"Thanks." Tru smiled to herself. So helpful she was.

Going into the first stall, she sat down on the commode and pulled out her gun. Never assume. That was the first thing she'd learned. Never assume that the person you were after didn't have a gun too. The toilet paper came rolling under the door just as the door to the bathroom closed.

Flushing and going to wash her hands, she kept an eye on the woman. She could do her in here, but then she'd have to figure out what to do with the body. Shaking the water off her hands, she made her way to the dryer when she came out of the stall.

"Mother fuck, it's hot out, isn't it? I had no idea it was this hot when we decided this would be a good place to retire. Are you here on vacation?" She mumbled about working but didn't expect her to care anyway. "Bob and I, we're here hiding out for a week or two. Until things die down. Got us a mess in the States that we should have been smarter about."

Tru pretended to be interested. All the while, she was thinking that this woman was stupider than she'd been informed. Where the hell did she think she was but in the United States? Or did she think that California was a country all on its own? As she told Tru about the mess in the States, Rogen spoke to her through their link.

I'm to tell you that if you want to take care of her in the bathroom, you only need to unlock the window. Is there one in there large enough to get her through? Tru told her there was and that she was telling her all about her problems. *I heard that she wasn't one to keep her mouth shut. All right. You take her out, and then someone will come in and get the body. I'm supposed to remind you that you're to lock the door. Like you'd forget something like that.*

I'll do it as I'm pretending the leave. This place, this bar, what do you know about it? Other than what was on the paperwork? Rogen told her nothing, then asked her why. *I would think that someone as smart as you would know that this place is right now filled with at least three of the FBI's most wanted. And two more that I'm pretty sure I saw hanging on your wall. Of the fifteen people here, excluding me and Chatty Kathy here, there are fifteen wanted people. There are cameras.* Tru gave her the names of the two cameras she'd seen. She knew that Rogen had the best equipment and that her facial recognition would tell her who was who before she could figure it out on her own.

Got it. Well, well, you're so right. From what I can see over the last couple of days of films, the place seems to be the spot to go to if you're wanted. I can see that this place would be better, just gone. Hell, even the bartender is wanted for espionage. Tru was sort of sad to hear that. *Get out. Take her out or not, but get out. I have two flyers going by in about five to ten minutes.*

Moving out of the bathroom, she made sure that both

the male and female were still inside as she ticked away the time. Rogen warned her twice at the five minute mark and the one minute mark when she was down behind one of the closest buildings.

The building blew just as she said it would. Nothing else was targeted, and even the two cars out front of the place had minimal damage. They'd be trashed by the flames, but the rest of the street was safe. Moving toward the scene again, she kept up a running wealth of detailed information to Rogen about what she was seeing.

Crater sized hole. Both buildings on either side are up but will need to be taken down. Two bodies that were coming out are both dead. One of them lost most of their head. There is no smell of gas that I can detect. Also, there is a sublevel here that looks as if it was set up for some kind of overnighters. Perhaps a place for the hunted to lay low. She also told her of the conversation with the female about just that thing. *The alcohol is burning most of what the bomb didn't get. I'm not sure what they'll say when the police arrive, but I'm sure you have a handle on that.*

I do. Are you leaving tonight or in the morning? As far as anyone is going to be concerned, everyone, including you, was in the building when it blew. Don't go by the hotel if you're not staying. I'm making sure that you're beyond recognition now. She told her she was going to just see if she could get a flight out tonight then. *Good. They want you to go by DC if you can on your way back here.*

They both knew she would go straight home. Tru did work for the government, but she didn't want to do things that were out of the country anymore. Speaking to the president, she knew he'd talk her into coming to work for him on all grounds.

No one knew that she and Rogen had their own way of keeping in touch with each other. It made it nice, Tru thought, to be able to talk to someone when she needed information without having to figure out a burner phone and what to do with it when she was finished.

As she was moving out of the way of the firetruck, she saw the male moving among the rest of the site seers.

We have an issue. Rogen asked her what it was. After telling her, Rogen asked after the female. *He's alone. Covered in blood. I don't know where she is, but I'm working my way toward him. If I see her, she'll be taken care of as well.*

Rogen wouldn't bother her again unless she spoke first. Tru would need to focus on what her task was and make sure she did her job. As soon as she came upon the male—he was leaning over and puking his guts up—she shot him once in the back of the head. He fell forward, landing nicely in his own vomit. Moving out of the way, she saw her other target. Waiting for her to check to see if the male was all right—he'd fallen to his knees and stayed there—Tru shot her too.

Blending into the crowd again, she told Rogen where the bodies were. Tru watched two men come out of the shadows and pick them both up, tossing them over their shoulders as they jogged up the sidewalk. No one took any notice of them, as they were too fixated on the building burning in front of them.

That was another perk that she enjoyed working directly with Rogen. There was no need for her to do a clean up when she was out. Rogen had stashes of people all over the world for just that purpose. And if they weren't that close, she'd have them there. Just a couple of people to pick up the bodies and make sure that the room or whatever was just as un-bloodied as it had been before she entered.

Sitting on the plane, waiting to get going, the pilot came over the PA and said that they were going to be delayed for several minutes. He was sorry and blah, blah, blah. She saw the Secret Service moving toward where she was sitting. Cursing under her breath at the shit the president did to get someone's attention, she was glad she was still in disguise from her job.

There were six of them, all dressed in black, wearing masks over their faces as well as their weapons out at their chest. The single man, dressed as the others but with no gun out, asked if she'd come with them.

"Are you asking me or telling me?" He just smiled at her. "I guess you think that's supposed to be a fucking answer?"

"We'd very much like for you to come with us to the front of the plane and out, Agent one seven four eight." She growled low and knew that he heard it. "The president would like a word or two with you, and he said to tell you that this way you won't have to go see him first before going home."

"I think you're well aware that I wasn't going to talk

to him at all." He just smiled again. The woman sitting in the seat next to her gasped when she stood up. Her gun and holster were there for her to see. "It's all right, ma'am, I'm one of the good guys."

"Yes, that's what my husband used to say right before he'd blacken my eyes. Are you really supposed to go and talk to the president, young lady?" Tru said it didn't look as if he was giving her much of a choice. "You tell him for Mary Conley that he's doing a damned sight better job now that he's got his head out of his ass and is paying attention to things around him. You tell him that for me."

"I promise you, I will."

She was escorted out of the plane and up the runway. She didn't speak to the people around her. They'd not answer her questions anyway. But she did reach out to Rogen and told her what the fucker was doing to her. *I want to make sure he knows better than to do this again. I'm still armed, and I'd like to make my own little statement right now.*

I'm glad to help. She could almost feel Rogen's humor about what was going to go down. *All right. The limo is out front. I've looked, and there doesn't appear to be anyone in it but the driver. If you're going to do something, I'd suggest you do it before you get out of the airport. After that, I will only be able to keep track of you and not help you out of the building.*

Deal.

She pretended to twist her ankle and fell to the floor. In doing so, she took out the two men following her. Knocking them both to the floor, she was able to disarm one of them and use the gun on the second one. They were wearing vests, but at the close range, it caused them enough pain to have them out when she shot them both. With the trash can that was close to her, Tru hit the other two. Using her body, a lethal weapon she'd been told, Tru was able to not just take their guns from them, but she had one locked in her legs until he was out before she shot the other man in the chest with the gun right up to the chest plate he was wearing. All that was left was the smiler.

"You don't want to do this." She said that she really did. That he'd forced her hand. "Look. We'll just get in the car, and I'll brief you before we get there."

"That's all? You're going to take me all by yourself without all the firepower?" He said he promised. "All right then. I'm trusting you."

She took his hand in hers and saw the cuffs before he got them on her wrists. Tru knew he wasn't to be trusted any more than she was. Hitting him in the face with her foot, the man was out before he hit the floor. She put the cuffs on him and one of the downed men before getting the others trussed up too.

All right. Get me out of here in one piece. Rogen was laughing, so she was sure she'd watched her on the camera. Moving in the direction that Rogen told her, she laughed again when Rogen mentioned that she didn't want to be on her bad side. *You get me out of here, and we'll talk about it.*

Discarding the wig and other items that changed her

features, she was pleased that Rogen not only got her out of the building but had a car waiting for her at the car rental place. Getting in it, she was glad that it wasn't some fuddy duddy car, but something she could have a little fun with. Before starting it, however, she did ask her who was paying for it.

It's a freebie, of course. When you get to the end of the lot, pull over. There are several tracking devices on that sucker that you need to disarm.

After getting the car clean, Tru was on her way home. The only way they'd be able to find her now was if they knew that she had rented a car and under whose name. The funny thing was, no one had rented this car, and no one had paid for it. Rogen had taken it off their books and inventory. No one would know that the thing was missing, as it was never there. She loved her job.

Chapter 10

Jonas waited at the door for his brother to come and see the kids. He didn't know when they'd gotten sick, but two of them had been throwing up since he arrived. The other two, including the baby, were sleeping whatever it was off. The sitter was missing too.

"Thank goodness." Dawson asked him where the kids were. "There are two in the bedroom sleeping. They don't have a temperature, but they're sticky with sweat."

He examined the two that he'd put in the living room with buckets. After they answered questions put to them, Jonas went to the other two children. Bobby was awake, but he didn't feel good, he told him. Picking up the baby, Jonas changed her out of her wet sleeper and was worried that her urine was so dark. Dawson came in to check on them when he sat in the rocker to rock Sarah.

"Food poisoning is my first guess." He said that's what he thought as well. "Isn't there an adult here with them?"

"I'm having someone find her." Dawson checked Sarah, who was crying but not sweating anymore. "They were alone when I arrived. Thomas told me that Cindy left them two days ago and hadn't returned. She'd better have a fucking good excuse for leaving them like this."

"They need to be with someone all the time right now, Jonas. Do you have anyone else that can look after them for you?" He said he was doing it for now. "Four sick kids are going to be hard on you. I don't know if you know this or not, but if this is food poisoning, it will be a couple of days before any of them will be well enough to take any fluids in. I'm concerned for their wellbeing. Not that I don't think you could do it, but you do need some help."

"I have to keep them safe, Dawson. I made a promise to them." Dawson told him that he could take them back with him to the family, and they'd make sure they were safe and getting better. "I've been thinking about that. But logistically, I haven't any way of doing that with four of them."

"I'm calling Mom. That is if you don't mind. You know as well as I do that she'll have them home with soup in their bellies before either one of us can figure out even getting a car seat for them in a car." Dawson was right. Jonas knew it. But he didn't want his family to know about this or some of the other things he was into. "What do you want to do?"

"Call her for me, please." Jonas had been there since midnight when Thomas had called him. Bobby was throwing up, and he could hear the baby screaming her head off. He was in the car and going to them even before Thomas hung up the phone.

Mom wanted to talk to him, so he handed Sarah off to his brother as he took the phone. He just didn't want her to be yelling at him at the moment and started out saying that to her.

"Why would you assume I was going to be upset with you?" He said that he was sorry and exhausted. "I'm sure you are. Dawson said they were ill and that he was going to run some blood work on them. We're coming there to help you now. I'd rather bring them here if you'd not mind."

"No, I think that would be the best place for them." He moved out of the bedroom into the kitchen, where the kids couldn't hear him. "Mom, they've been badly abused. Thomas won't allow anyone to touch him but me. Not even his brother and sisters. Sarah is terrified of the dark and needs to have a light on all the time. Hailey won't eat anything unless she sees you take it out of the package and watches it being prepared. Bobby is…he's broken, Mom. I mean that literally. His arm and leg are in casts. There are wounds on his back that he won't tell me where they came from. Not only does he look like someone put cigarettes out on his back and belly, but they might well have used his mouth as an ashtray too."

"Oh, Jonas. Those poor children. My heart hurts for them. Where is this monster that did this to them?" He told her that he was taken care of. "The mother? What is her role in all of this?"

"Margo is a junkie and a whore. When the kids were being taken care of by their father while she was in jail, this was done to them. Margo is aware that he's hurt them, but not to what extent. She's not ever going to get them unless she kills me first." Mom, his wonderful mom, said she wasn't getting them over her dead body either. "I'm sorry to have sprung this on you like this. The kids have been in my care for a few weeks now. I didn't want to involve you guys, as you all seem to be busy with other stuff. But I'm so glad that Dawson told me I needed help. I think I have known that for a while now but was too stupid to ask for it."

"You're never stupid for helping out someone that needs it, Jonas. Never forget that. You needed to figure it out on your own that you needed us. I hope the next time you save a family, you remember to let us help you. All right, son, Thatcher and your dad are on the way with the van." He thanked her again. "I'm making some chicken and dumplings for the little ones. If you'd join us for dinner, we can sort things out."

"All right, Mom. Thank you so much." Mom told him she'd see him soon, and he hung up the phone. The knock at the door had him telling everyone to be quiet. He looked out the peephole and saw the police there. Opening the door, he was surprised when they asked him if he was Jonas Robinson. "I am. What's happened?"

"Cindy James, she works for you?" He said that she did. "I'm sorry to tell you, sir, but she was killed yesterday. It took us until today to figure out who she was. I'm afraid that whoever killed her, they didn't take care for us to be able to identify her easily. She was torn up badly, and it was difficult to even see that she was a female when they were finished."

"How did you know to find me here?" The other officer handed him a cell phone in an evidence bag. It was covered in blood, and the screen was broken. His picture was there, as well as his phone number. She called him boss and nothing more. "That still doesn't tell me how this led you to here."

"Agent Rogen Robinson, she's your sister-in-law? After it was put on the news with your picture, she called us. She also took the news program off the air. I don't know how she was able to do that, but she said you were to be contacted in person." Jonas owed her for that. "She gave us the address where the phone was last used. You sure do have some good people in your corner, young man."

"I do." His dad and brother showed up then, and he told them what was going on. "I'm taking the children to my family's home. I'd appreciate it if you didn't put this address or my name anywhere it can be traced."

"Agent Robinson said that she'd have our asses for lunch if we even wrote a note about a thing that we've done today. I believe her too." Jonas said he was smart in that. "We're also to assist you in any way you need. Again without making any notes. She sure is intense, isn't she?"

"You have no idea."

The officers helped them bundle up the children as well as pack up their clothing. Jonas contacted Rogen as he was in the bathroom gathering up toothbrushes and such. *How much do I owe you for saving my ass?*

I'll have to give that some thought. I do want to tell you that your Cindy didn't go easy. She suffered more than I've seen in a long time. Since they didn't find you there, I can only assume that she didn't tell whoever took her anything. By the way, she was headed out to get some clear soda for the kids. It was found not far from her body with the receipt inside the bag.

What do you know about what happened? I've not done anything to anyone but Margo, and I doubt very much she'd be sober or straight enough to know how to hurt someone. Rogen told him it was a professional. *You mean as a hit? Who would do that? I'm assuming it has something to do with the kids.*

I'm still looking. There are a couple of things I need to ask you when you get here. Also, I've hired a few people to tail you home and watch the place when you leave. I don't know that Cindy told them anything, but I won't take that chance with those kids. He thanked her. *No need for that, Jonas. You're a good man.*

Can you do me a favor? Margo claims that she has a brother, someplace. I have no idea if that's a fabrication on her part or not, but his name is Benson. That's all I know. Last name is either Whitman or Winterman. She wasn't sure either. Rogen laughed. *I know. How could you forget your own brother's name? Anyway, he might well have washed his hands of his sister and will take the kids as his own. I don't care one way or the other. I'll adopt them myself if it comes to that.*

Rogen said she'd do that now. After closing the connection with her, he was ready to get the kids into the van. There was a meltdown from Thomas when Dad tried to help him into the van seat. It took them an extra twenty minutes or so to calm him down. Even then, he was still crying. Hailey didn't want to get into the car seat. He finally had to have Dawson give both Thomas and Hailey something to calm them down.

Jonas wanted to cry. He wasn't a whiny person, and he thought of himself as being made of stronger stuff. But this was stressing him out to the limit. It was Dad that took him aside and told him to get himself home by running as his tiger.

"I can't do this to you guys. You've seen how upset they are." Dad told him they could more than likely feel his stress too. "I'm upsetting them?"

"Yes. You don't have to talk to see that you're upset. You're doing a good job of being a good man to them. But like all kids, they know. You just get yourself on home and let your cat out for a while. Nothing calms me faster than a good run. You'll see, son, they'll be right as rain when we get them to your momma." He didn't want to, but he knew he wasn't his usually quiet self around the kids. Too much, he told himself. "Go on now. You go to the house, and we'll be there soon. You'll feel better for it."

He did what his dad suggested. Jonas did feel better

when he got home. Mom had been waiting for him with some clothes, so he was ready to deal with the kids better when they arrived. The entire house smelled like chicken soup. It was enough to make him feel like he was doing the right thing in bringing them all here to be with his family.

Sitting Bobby on one of the kitchen chairs with his leg propped up, he told his mom that he could eat a little. That he was feeling better. Sarah was holding onto Jonas tight enough that he was sure she was going to leave marks. It wasn't until Allie and Beck showed up that she let Beck hold her. Thomas was still sleeping off the medication that Dawson had given him, and Hailey watched his mom preparing the soup. He was surprised when she asked for a bottle of water. Then she ate the soup. Jonas was so happy that he did a little jig.

Rogen joined them just as Thomas was waking up. She took one look at Bobby and asked him if he was all right. When the little boy dropped his head, Rogen pulled it back up and looked at him.

"When I ask you something, I'd like an answer, if you don't mind." He told her he was sorry. "Why? Because some fucktard hurt you? You have nothing to be sorry for, Bobby. You were hurt by a monster, and from what I understand, he won't touch you again."

"No ma'am. Mr. Jonas said he'd keep us safe from them." She asked who they were. "Our mom. She's mean too, but she never hurt us like Dad did. Mr. Jonas has been really good to us."

"He's a man you can trust." Bobby looked at him. "All of us are going to keep you safe, Bobby. And when I mean safe, I also mean we'll make sure you have food and clothing and that no one will touch you again. Do you believe me?"

Bobby looked at his sisters and brother before looking at Jonas. He told him he would keep them safe, but as Rogen said, they'd help too. Before Bobby spoke again, he leaned back in his seat. Of all four of the kids, Bobby was the most outspoken.

"If I tell you something, something important, will you help us still?" She told him there were no conditions on her helping them. She'd do it anyway. "I'm going to trust you with something that will get us in big trouble. You too, if anyone finds out. Okay?"

"Bobby, we made a promise." Bobby told Thomas that they needed help. "I know, but we made a promise. And she told us that it would come back on us if we told anyone."

"I think you need to tell me, boys. If it's going to be bad, I'll be able to help you more if I know what I'm up against." Bobby asked Thomas what he wanted to do, and when he nodded, Jonas let out the breath he was holding. "All right now? You're willing to tell me?"

"Yes, ma'am." He took a bit of the soup on his spoon and sipped it noisily. When he laid the spoon back on the table, he looked directly at him. "My dad robbed a man of all his drugs. He told us that he was going to be rich and he'd be able to have better kids. We told Mom what he'd said, but we lied and told her that we didn't know where it was. Thomas and I do. We know where it is because we moved it after Mom got arrested."

"Is it a lot of drugs, Bobby?" He nodded. "Tell me how much. Like bigger than this table? Would it fit on the table?"

"It won't fit in this room." Jonas was glad that he was sitting down. He didn't know what the kids had done to move a room full of drugs, but he was sure it would get them killed. "We had to move it, Mr. Jonas. Some bad people were going to sell it to everyone, and they'd die. That's what Dad told us. That the drugs were spoiled and would kill anyone who took it."

"Christ." He had to agree with Rogen on that. "All right. You tell me where it is, and I'll make sure it's taken care of."

"I will, but…will you promise to help us when you get it? Dad said people would do anything for the amount of drugs that was there. Kill for it even." They all swore that they'd take care of them forever if it came to that. "Just be careful. Okay?"

"Yes, you can count on us all being careful." Bobby and Thomas told them where they could find the drugs. Not only that but where they'd gotten it from too. Rogen shook Bobby's hand and told Thomas that she was happy they'd told them. "Bobby, you and Thomas have done a good thing with this. I'm very proud of you."

He knew that Rogen would get right on retrieving the drugs. But she stayed to talk to the kids a little more.

Even Thomas loosened up a little around her. Sarah was still clinging to Beck, but she did watch Rogen closely.

Jonas didn't ask her how she was going to get to the drugs. Nor did he wonder if she would. It would be just a matter of her calling in someone to get it and figure out who it had been taken from. He had a feeling that was why Cindy had been murdered.

~*~

Benson put the phone back in the cradle. Shivering at what had been told to him, he looked up when his wife came into the room. He told her that he'd just gotten a call from the FBI, that his sister's kids needed them to come and get them.

"All right. When are we leaving?" He told Sissy that they weren't going to. "What do you mean we're not going to go get them? They're your family, Benny. You can't just leave them in the hands of others. Of course, you want to go get them."

"What if they're, you know, colored?" She asked him what he'd said. "You know my sister. She's nothing but a sleaze bag. She's more than likely slept with everything with a dick. I'm betting animals too. I don't want a colored kid in my house. And you shouldn't either if you know what's good for you."

"I cannot believe you just said that. You are seriously messed up if you think skin color or anything else matters when it comes to family." He said that people would stare at them. "So? Since when do you give a shit what people think when they see you? If you did, then you'd clean up better and lose some weight."

"You're talking shit, Sissy, and you know how much I hate that." She lifted her chin to him, and he was tempted as hell to knock her block off. "I made you a promise that I'd never hit you again, but you're pushing me. Really pushing me."

"You touch me, Benson Whitman, and I'll put you in a world of hurt so bad that you'll never be able to come up for air again." He was tempted. The first time he'd hit her, the only time as it turned out, she'd done so much to him that he was still feeling the repercussions from it.

He didn't have a job and couldn't get one. Well, he supposed he could get a job, but he wasn't going to work a job that was beneath him. There wasn't a car for him to use anymore, as she'd sold his. Benny had looked for three days for her car and given up. He was, he knew, too lazy to put too much effort into much of anything. Then there was the fact that she'd had him beaten up. She said that she'd not done that, but he knew it could only have been her.

"We're going to go and get those kids." He forgot, just for a moment, that he no longer ruled the house. That he wasn't in charge. When his fist connected with her face and she fell over, he knew he'd just fucked himself over double time, and then some.

Leaving the house before she woke up, he didn't even have to look in Sissy's purse to know that there'd be no money for him to take. She hid that from him as well. Not that either of them had all that much. But she made it a point to keep whatever she had away from him.

Benny made his way to the only place he knew he'd feel welcome. The Community Bar. Dumbest name for a bar he'd ever heard, but it was always full, and there was always someone that would buy him a beer or two just to keep him from singing. Benny couldn't hold a tune in a bucket with the lid glued down, as his granny used to tell him. Going inside, he wondered what he'd do if his wife just never got up. Never spoke to him like he was nothing again. It would be too good to be true; that's what it would be.

~*~

Sissy opened her eyes and didn't move. She wasn't sure if Benny was still there or not. If he was, she was going to murder his ass. Fucking bastard. Sitting up, letting her head figure out that it was still attached to her neck, she thought of what she had to do now.

She'd been so in love with Benson when she'd first met him. He'd been kind. Polite. He'd been such a dashing figure too. It only took her a few months to figure out he'd married her for money. Well, she nipped that in the bud right away.

The Morgans had money—a great deal of it. She did, as well. But as soon as she figured out Benny's scheme in trying to drain her dry, she told him she wasn't one of those Morgans, the ones with money. She was just plain old Sissy Morgan, who just happened to have the same last name as the rich ones. Her dad had helped her out with that as well.

"To think that I liked him." Sissy laughed with her dad when they plotted to have her husband think she was just as poor as he was. "Well, we'll get him on the right track soon enough. He might well give up if he figures out that he should love you, not what you have."

"I hope so, Dad."

As it turned out, he only loved what she could have given him. It had taken her another four years to harden her heart against him. To turn what could have been the most monumental love that had ever been created into nothing more than tolerance and disdain. Hitting her today was going to cost him more than he figured she had in her bank accounts when she'd met him.

Gathering up what she needed, Sissy called the police. As soon as she had them on the phone, she told them what had happened. Since her family pretty much funded all their endeavors when it came to food and toy drives, she knew they'd come right away. She also told them where her soon to be ex-husband would be.

Then she called her dad. "He's hit me again." Dad told her he'd be right over. "I'm going to go to the hospital so they can take pictures and record what he's done to me. Can you just meet me there?"

She felt her eyes well up with tears when her dad told her how much he loved her. "Honey, I'm going to call Ginger too. It's time for her to come home anyway. Once she's here, we'll band up together and take care that he gets what he deserves." She told him she didn't want to bother her sister. "She's going to be mighty upset when she figures out what you've been through, don't you think?"

"Yes. She's always been my protector. But she also has a life that she loves, Dad. She'll come home, but I know she'll just be gone again when she starts that itchy thing she calls her job." They both laughed. "All right. Call her, but don't let on that I'm upset or anything. Just tell her what's going on and let her decide if she wants to come back here or not."

Sissy decided that she wasn't going to tell her dad about her sister-in-law and her children. If she could convince Ginger to go with her, then that would be that. Sissy had always wanted a large family. This would be the best way to get one without having a man hanging around all the time. Sitting in the chair when she'd gotten all her things gathered up, Sissy called the locksmith to have every lock on the property changed out. He wasn't going to get to sleep in the fucking shed if she could do something to keep him from it.

The police showed up when the ambulance did. She answered all their questions and asked a few of her own. Yes, he'd been picked up. And no, she'd have to press charges herself or get her attorney to do so. Calling Dad while they were loading her in the ambulance, she asked him to call Mr. Beagle. He said he'd get right on it.

By the time her dad showed up, she'd had X-rays showing that she had a concussion. Also, they'd put fifty-four stitches in the back of her head where she'd hit something on her way down, and twelve on her face where he'd not just busted open her lips, but her cheek as well. The doctor told her it was a good thing she had a hard head, or it might have been a lot worse than it was.

"I've left a message for Ginger at the last place I heard from her. The man that answered said that she was going to be gone and without cell service for another few days, but he'd have her call." Dad pulled his pillow out of his bag he'd brought. "I don't want to hear a thing about me not staying. If I were to go home, all I'd do is sit up and worry. You and Ginger are all I have in the world, and I won't be fine with one of you laid up in the hospital."

"I'm glad to have you here, Dad." They didn't talk much. Her head was pounding now, and she asked for something for the pain. Once they gave her that, she was able to relax more and tell him what she wanted to do. "I've thought about this a great deal, so I'm set up so that he can't take more from me. I still laugh when I think of you getting him to sign that prenup when we were married. You telling him that I might win the lottery someday was the funniest thing you could have said to him. Especially since I've never bought a lottery ticket in my life."

"I thought he was just being funny when I think about his comment. But now that I've seen the man in action, I think he's stupider than a bag of rocks. My goodness, he surely did let himself go, didn't he?" She told her dad that he was also a diabetic. "And him down there at the bar drinking. There isn't any help for people like him. You tell them and tell them, and it goes in one ear and right out the other." Dad laughed. "I've been reading again. Some of them old books sure do have a saying for just about any situation."

When she was feeling just a little better, she told her dad that she was going to try and get some sleep. Her head was still hurting, but not enough where it would keep her up. As she was dozing off, she heard her dad on the phone. While she wanted to ask him what was going on, she was too far gone to do so. Dad, her dad, could handle just about anything.

Chapter 11

Beck stood back and watched the lines he was sure the problem was coming from. Everything else that he'd tried kept having him end up here at the merge of the three lines together. He wouldn't have done that, have three major lines meet in one place, but it seemed to be working well until the last couple of months.

I have two questions for you, then I'll try not to bother you again. He smiled and told Allie that he liked her kind of interruptions. *Thanks. I needed that. What do you know about a company named Hershel's Baskets?*

Nothing more than I've seen on television or in the paper. They make and deliver gift baskets, correct? She said they delivered them, but they didn't make the baskets. *Is that important? I mean, I'm sure that there are several companies out there that don't make the gift baskets they fill.*

This company claims they make them. And it's a sticking point for a lot of people wanting to sue them. I have no idea why that matters — like you said, there are plenty of other companies out there that don't make their baskets. He asked her what was going on. *I'm doing another local job. Although this is far from local. The company is out west in California, and the police there heard that I could figure out crime scenes. That's the second question I have for you. The first one was just a curiosity. The second question. Have you ever eaten or heard of head cheese?*

I don't think so. I mean, with a name like that, it doesn't sound all that appetizing. It's not made with heads, is it? She said that it actually was—pig head parts. *Then absolutely not—I've not eaten any.* He thought for a moment. *Please tell me that is another curiosity question, and this place isn't making this out of human heads.*

They are, from what I can figure out. The police are still searching for ten to a thousand homeless. Don't get me started on why the numbers are that far apart. They don't keep track, they told me. Anyway, they sent the stuff in to be analyzed—just for fun, they told me—and it came back with human DNA in it. Like ninety percent of the shit is human. Beck felt his belly lurch a little. *After it came back marked with several different DNA in it, the police didn't have any idea where to go from there. It has them stalemated, I was told. They've not only not arrested anyone, but they've not gone there to find out what the fuck is going on either. Like they're afraid they might well have eaten their brothers or something.*

That's the grossest thing I've ever heard of. She said there was more. *I don't want you to share. Please. Oh, Christ, that's disgusting.*

The other three here got sick from it too. Just thinking

about it. I'm the outside the box thinker in this, and I'm too curious to figure out how they did it rather than be grossed out about it. So I'm going to go there in about an hour to have a tour. I'm taking not just your dad, but Thatcher and Dawson are going with me too. We are going to be seeing how the place cooks up this head stuff. He asked her if Dad or the others knew what they were going there to find. *Thatcher and Dawson know. Your dad doesn't. Someone needs to be shocked when we find out — if we find out what they're doing. All I can think about is that soylent green movie.*

Now that was all he could think about. Laughing a little with her, he asked her if any police were going with them. She told him that Rogen was watching on a camera that they were all wearing. Also, of course, that she'd hacked into their system. Beck wondered why she'd not been able to find it if she had their cameras.

I asked her too. She said there is one part of the building that she can't get into. No cameras. I don't know how she figures we're going to get in there, but I'm giving it my best shot. How are you doing there? Find the trouble? He said he was narrowing it down. *I hope you remember you need to be home by Saturday. Conor has his physical, and he won't let me go with him. Also, Jonas needs you to help him close up a couple of homes he is working on.*

I have it on my calendar. I won't forget. He was actually looking forward to having some time with Conor. *I'm planning to leave here as soon as I get this figured out.*

Good. He could feel her hesitating and waited. *If they're using an infrared reader on the boxes, look around the clogging area for a mirror. Or something equally shiny. Something that might reflect back the lights and mess with the reader. I've seen that happen before.*

It only took him ten minutes to find the reflection. It was a mirror on the bathroom doorway, where a person could look at themselves for having things put back together properly after using the facility. It was newly installed and doing just what she said it was doing. Reflecting the reader back onto itself and giving a bad read.

It took him another hour and a half to get the management to see it was their problem and that it needed to be removed. By the time he left the plant, he was ready to murder someone. Who would have thought they'd have to call a board meeting to take a mirror down? He was half tempted to just paint over it himself. Save the glass and perhaps seven years of bad luck.

Driving home, he wasn't in any kind of hurry. Allie and his family had left already, and he decided he wanted to spend some quality time with his mom. Calling her up, he first asked her where she was. If she was at one of her many committee meetings, he was going to beg off. He hated going to those things.

"I was just sitting here, contemplating if I wanted lunch or not. Your dad is off with Allie and Thatcher. I didn't want to go with them." Beck asked her if she'd like to have lunch with her favorite son. "I told you, Beck, Thatcher has gone with your dad."

"Funny." She laughed with him. "I can come by

and pick you up, or if you're out already, we can meet someplace. The sky's the limit, my dear mom. Where would you like to go with your not so favorite son?"

Laughing still, she told him where she would meet him. After getting them a table, he watched the crowd of people as they picked up their lunch and left again. There wouldn't be too many more days like this one. The fall leaves were just beginning to turn, and he loved the crispness of the air.

Mom kissed him on the cheek when she sat down. She started talking about her garden almost as soon as she got her sweater off. Beck loved his mom and wished that he'd remembered to pick her up some flowers. When she slowed down in her report to him, Mom smiled hugely at him.

"What are you up to while your wife is gone?" He said he had plans with Conor. "I so love that boy. And Holly is a rare treat too. She's not very shy, is she? But Conor, he's still adjusting, and my heart hurts for him."

"Since he's been going to practice after school, he's calmed down a great deal. I think he wasn't used to having so much free time. They were forever trying to get something to eat. He's been hanging out with Bobby too. Helping him get around and such. Thomas too. The three of them have had a harder life than most people I know."

"Yes, I agree with you there. That Hailey is so quiet and scares me at times. Not that I think she'll harm me, but she seems to look right into your heart when she's watching you. The other day I made the mistake of handing her a glass of water. She didn't say anything but dumped it into the sink. I wonder if she'll ever trust anyone again." Beck asked her if she wanted to know the story behind her mistrust. "I believe it has something to do with her mother trying to kill her off. I don't know why that thought is circling around my head."

"Not her mom, but her father. He tried to give her something that would knock her out. She was keeping the baby safe, and when he knocked her out the one time, Sarah had been beaten up. Apparently, she was crying from teething and wouldn't quiet down when her father wanted to take a snooze. Jonas told me." Mom asked him if he thought Jonas would adopt them. "I do. He's been looking into it since he's been keeping them safe. I want him to do it too. I think they trust him more than anyone else they are around. Including any of us."

"He's going to have his hands full, but I think if anyone can do it, it would be him. He's not afraid to say he needs help. Jonas has always been like that." Beck knew that about his little brother. "Anyway, I was thinking about the holidays yesterday. I've decided I need to give away some of my Christmas decorations. I have so many now that I can't put even a quarter of it out. But when I find it at an auction, I just can't turn it down for a few dollars."

"Yes, you can, Mom. In fact, I think it's easier to just walk away from it." She smacked him on the hand. After they ordered, he told her what he thought she should do with it all. "Just take it to one of the empty buildings we own and let us go over it to see if we want any. Then, if you don't care if you make anything from it, give it to anyone that wants it. Let them decorate their yard for a change."

"I've donated so much to the Salvation Army. Did you know that they just give things away that are donated? I like that very much. Last year I was able to get them twenty trees that they used to give to people that just don't have the money to get one." He told her he'd always known his mom was special. "Thank you, son. I love you very much, as well."

As they were walking around their little town, he and his mom were stopped no less than a dozen times. Mr. Chablis asked if the two of them had a few minutes. He wanted to ask them something.

"Usually, I just toss this stuff on the fire and say I got suckered. But I thought of you when I realized what I have here." As they were headed to the backroom, Beck asked him what he'd done. "I buy up bulk items. Sometimes there isn't all that much I can use. Other times I find things that go with pieces I already have. It's fun for me. Your mom can usually find someone to take the toys off my hands when I get them up and running. But this box has something I didn't expect. Wrapping paper."

It wasn't just a box of wrapping paper that one might pick up at a store, but a pallet loaded up with hundreds of brand new boxes of it. All Christmas, from what he could see, as well as a variety of scenes that he thought were very festive. He asked Mr. Chablis what he wanted to do with them.

"I was thinking of donating it to your mom so she can make sure it gets into the right hands." Beck told him what he and his mom had discussed. "I like that idea. That's brilliant. I have some Christmas items back in the storage barn too. This might well be a good way for me to clear out some room. I've been meaning to get it out anyway."

"I can help you with taking it over to the building. All of us will." Mr. Chablis was ready to start moving it right now; he was so excited. "I'll get with my brothers, and we'll get back to you. This will be so helpful to the town, I think. Mom, you're the best."

After leaving the secondhand shop, he and Mom talked about what they were going to do when they got things organized. He was excited too. Giving back was something that he enjoyed more than anything, especially at Christmas time.

Beck was just getting himself some dinner when he heard from Allie. He'd not bothered her much today, knowing that she was figuring something out. But she sounded so distressed that he put his sandwich on hold and paid attention to what she was telling him.

We've found the room where they're making the headcheese, Beck. It's terrible. I thought for sure that your dad was going to kill the men working there. He asked her if she was all right. *No. Not at all. It's a lot worse than we thought. I'm not going into details because my mind is still wrapping around what we found. But could you come out here? I need you in the worst sort of way.*

I'm going to leave right now. He went up to his room to pack and decided that he could purchase what he would need. *I'm going to be there in a few hours, honey. Then we'll just sit around and talk about anything but what you found.*

He was nearly to the airport when he realized he wanted to bring the kids. Going back home, he called the packhouse and asked to speak to Conor and Holly. Both wanted to go with him, and Conor said he'd get his physical when they got back. That Mom — he called them Mom and Dad now — needed them more than he needed football.

He was glad that he'd thought about them the moment they were in the car with him. These kids were theirs, and perhaps while they were out there, he'd show them a good time. Yes, Beck thought, kids were the greatest.

Before You Go...

HELP AN AUTHOR

write a review

THANK YOU!

Share your voice and help guide other readers to these wonderful books. Even if it's only a line or two, your reviews help readers discover the author's books so they can continue creating stories that you'll love. Log in to your favorite retailer and leave a review. Thank you.

AWARD WINNING, BESTSELLING AUTHOR

Kathi Barton, a winner of the Pinnacle Book Achievement award as well as a best-selling author on Amazon and All Romance books, lives in Nashport, Ohio, with her husband, Paul. When not creating new worlds and romance, Kathi and her husband enjoy camping and going to auctions. She can also be seen at county fairs with her husband, who is an artist and potter.

Her muse, a cross between Jimmy Stewart and Hugh Jackman, brings her stories to life for her readers in a way that has them coming back time and again for more. Her favorite genre is paranormal romance, with a great deal of spice. You can visit Kathi online and drop her an email if you'd like. She loves hearing from her fans. aaronskiss@gmail.com.

Follow Kathi on her blog: http://kathisbartonauthor. blogspot.com/

www.ingramcontent.com/pod-product-compliance
Lightning Source LLC
Chambersburg PA
CBHW020622180626
46810CB00007B/2897